WHEN A ROSE FALLS

Book One of the Briar Series

G. L. Strong

ISBN:9798428648799
Imprint: Independently Published

Thank you to all of my family and friends who have supported me through the ups and downs, late nights, and minor break downs that are involved in writing a book. I will forever be grateful for all of you.

PROLOGUE

Have you ever closed your eyes and imagined yourself as someone else? Someone prettier... skinnier... smarter? Just simply... better? You close your eyes and this version of yourself that is completely different appears. This confident, happy girl splays across the back of your eyelids smiling back at you... mocking you. Because she's not you. No, the you that exists wears all black. She barely speaks to anyone due to her crippling social anxiety. She has boring brown hair and stale blue eyes filled with shadows. It's been so long since she smiled that the movement alone strains the muscles in her face. She has demons so dark, that the devil himself would run in fear. That girl is the you that the world gets to see, while the beautiful happy bitch on the back of your eyelids hides away.

Well, at least that's how it is for me. Because I'm that stale, blue eyed girl.

CHAPTER 1

Charlotte

I'm staring up at my ceiling when my alarm goes off bringing me back to reality. The deafening blare cuts out when I push stop on my phone. An involuntary groan escapes me as I throw the blankets off my tired body. Sleep was not my friend last night. Not that it is most nights, with my nightmares invading every corner of my mind. You'd think after ten years they wouldn't affect me, but no amount of time seems to help me sleep through the memories.

After changing into my favorite black jeans, my black doc martens, and a matching black t-shirt, I take a look at the girl staring back at me in the mirror. My hair manages to be a frizzy, wavy mess while also lying flat and dull at the same time, reaching my lower back. The small freckles spattering my face remind me of specks of dirt that I wish I could rub away with the back of my hand. I'm average height with curves in all the wrong places.

With a sigh, I turn away and grab my bag off the floor, heading out my bedroom door. I can hear loud, raspy snoring coming from the living room downstairs. That snore belongs to my Uncle Brian, who probably just got home and is knocked out on the couch. He's been my legal guardian since I was eight years old, but he's definitely not parent material. He sleeps most of the day and works all night as a bartender. He tends to drink on the job, so we end up moving around a lot to find work. He's actually a really good uncle, his life just isn't what he thought it would be. He was only 21 when he got custody of me, and not much has changed in the ten years we've been together besides our mailing address.

I look down at him and cringe at the sight. He used to look like the traditional college frat boy; big muscles, bigger ego, and a permanent cocky smile. But, with age, and about 140 pounds of baggage named Charlotte, he has withered away into the man I see in front of me. Beer belly from too much drinking, worry lines permanently etched on his face, and way too much gray hair for a 31 year old.

Per usual I grab the blanket off the back of the couch and drape it over his body. On my way out the door, I grab a banana for my walk to school. Oh yeah, I forgot to mention today was my first day at a new school… at the end of the school year… my senior year. What could go wrong? I already know how it will go. I will blend into the background and no one will even realize I'm there. Which is exactly how I like it. I used to be the most talkative kid, always surrounded by friends. But, since *that* day, I have been a bit of a loner. I tend to get lost in my own head and zone out, which people apparently don't appreciate when they are talking to you.

The walk to school is about two miles long, but I don't care. Walking is the only thing that can clear my mind. The cool spring breeze, the birds chirping, the smell of fresh grass and flowers surrounding me. My senses are too overwhelmed for my demons to torment me.

All too soon, Pleasant Grove Heights comes into view and my heart starts racing involuntarily. The school is nicer than any of the other schools I've been to. It looks like a castle, with limestone walls cascading above the surrounding homes. It reminds me of Hogwarts, but in the middle of Vermont. I have no idea how my uncle can afford to stick me here for the next three months, but here I am nonetheless. The nerves bubbling up in my chest are making it tough to breathe. I stop in my tracks and take a few big deep breaths, scolding myself internally for getting this worked up over a new school. *Come on Charlie. It's just a school. A big, fancy, new school, but just a school. No one will notice you, you'll simply blend into the crowd.*

Taking one final deep breath, I continue walking until I'm at the black iron gate boasting the words *Pleasant Grove Heights* across the top. Checking my phone, I walk faster when I see that the time is 7:59 am, which is probably why there aren't any students outside the building right now. At the large wooden door, I take a deep breath again and grasp the handle before pulling hard. The door is heavy and creaks open, louder than I expect, so I slip in through the small crack instead of opening it all the way.

The noise is overwhelming to my ears. So many voices surround me as I take in the sight before me. The large hall goes on forever, with cathedral ceilings and dim lights lining the walls. The never ending hallway is also filled with students. Filled to the point that I can't move. Oh and the best part? They are all in the same outfit. Uniforms. Pleated skirts, khaki pants, white collared shirts, and matching burgundy ties are all I can see for what seems like miles. I'm frozen, debating on turning around and running before someone notices me. Right when I'm about to turn around, a bell rings and everyone starts to move and push past each other on their way to first period. Within minutes, I'm standing alone, my jagged breath echoing through the hall. *You got this Charlie. You can do it. Go find the office and they will get you a uniform and a schedule and everything will be fine.*

I start walking slowly, my steps loud in the silent hallway. Two doors down, I find a door that says 'Office' and open it, revealing a large room with three more doors, and a large desk in the middle of it. An elderly woman with glasses and a permanent scowl takes up the space behind the desk. When she hears me enter, she looks up at me and huffs loudly as she takes in my appearance.

"May I help you, miss?" her sharp voice makes me jump.

"Uh..." My voice comes out quiet and raspy. "Um, yeah... My name is Charlie, I'm-"

"Speak Up!" The woman glares at me as she scolds me.

"I'm sorry ma'am. My name is Charlie Briar. This is my first day at Pleasant Grove." I try to keep it together as this stranger stares at me disapprovingly. She looks over at the computer on her desk and starts typing away.

"I don't have a *Charlie* Briar in the system" She puts emphasis on the name Charlie. "But I have a Charlotte Briar."

"Yes, that's me. My name is Charlotte but I go by Charlie."

"Well, *Charlotte*, I have your schedule here but why are you not in your uniform?" She is holding my schedule hostage in her claw-like grasp until I answer her.

"I wasn't aware that there were uniforms ma'am. I don't have one."

The woman, Mrs. Burg, according to her desk placard, sighs in annoyance. "You get a pass today but tomorrow you need to arrive in the proper attire. A uniform was mailed to your residence. It should be there. We have arranged a student guide for you. They have the same schedule as you so you can stick together for the day until you are comfortable. He should be here soon. Please sit outside the office door on the bench and wait for him. *Quietly*." I nod my head as I grab the schedule and say thank you. She doesn't have to worry about me being loud.

I'd be happy if I didn't have to speak all day.

Spotting the bench outside the door, I plop down on it with a sigh. I hate meeting new people. I don't even see why I need a student guide, I am perfectly capable of walking around and finding a room number. And if I can't find the room, even better. I'll find the library, skip my classes, and read all day in a quiet corner all alone. I could live in a library. Just me and a million books surrounding me for the rest of time. The thought makes me snicker out loud as I look down at my hands and continue twisting my rings around my fingers, a nervous tick I picked up years ago. I'm so lost in my thoughts that I don't notice anyone walking towards me until I see two slightly scuffed brown oxford shoes standing right in front of me. *Shit. What would happen if I just didn't look up? Would he eventually walk away? If I don't move will he not see me? I think he already sees you Charlie. That's why he's standing two feet in front of you and-*

The sound of oxfords clearing his throat interrupts my thoughts and I know I am going to have to look up. My eyes slowly make their way up this stranger's body. The khaki pants that seem to go on forever, the tucked in white shirt that is perfectly ironed and stretched over what seem to be very muscular arms, and then I reach his face. *Holy hell.*

A pair of the sharpest green eyes stare back at me. They are the color of emeralds and the lashes that surround them are lush and thick. His brown hair is perfectly styled on top of his head and his skin looks like smooth porcelain. His lips are fastened in a cocky smirk which suddenly changes into an open mouthed smile revealing perfect white teeth. The sound of a husky laugh breaks me of my trance and I realize this guy is laughing at me. I look away from him as I feel my cheeks start to blush.

"Like what you see, new girl?"

He's making fun of me. Great, now I hate him and his stupidly handsome face. I stand up quickly and start to walk away. Where am I going? I have no clue. Maybe I can find the library.

"Hey wait, I'm sorry, I was just messing with you." I hear him jog to catch up with me. "I'm your guide, Paxton, but you can call me Pax." I don't slow down but he is right in line with me. He's a good foot taller than me so he has no problem keeping up with my shorter legs. "What's your name again?" His question hangs in the air with no response by me until his hand shoots out and touches my upper arm to stop me. The small gesture makes me gasp from the unexpected contact and I stop in my tracks.

I glare at him without truly meaning to. I'm not usually a mean person, I just don't like being touched and I don't want any friends.

"My name is Charlie. I don't need a guide, but thank you." I continue walking without giving him a chance to answer.

"Isn't Charlie a dude's name?" His voice right next to me makes me loudly huff and that earns me another laugh from oxfords.

"Yupp, it is. Now please leave me alone." I try to sound as nice as I possibly can, I promise.

"No can do Charlie. I was told to keep an eye on you at all times today, and I am not going to be on the other end of Mrs. Burg's wrath. She may be a little old secretary but she can be one scary ass woman. Which means, I can't lose sight of you today. But that won't be hard. You kinda stick out like a sore thumb in this school." His comment hits me hard and I stop walking. Now I'm getting annoyed.

"If I'm clearly so different than the rest of you rich kids then why don't you just leave me alone?" What has gotten into me today? Oxfords seems to bring out an angry side of me that I always keep hidden.

"Woah, woah, woah, I wasn't saying that. I only meant that everyone else is wearing white and red plaid uniforms and you're wearing all black." His defensive tone makes me look down at my own clothes and back up at his. *Shit.*

"Right…" I close my eyes for a second and take a deep breath. This is why I don't talk to people. When I open them back up, I see Paxton's bright green eyes sparkling at me and a big smile on his face. "Why are you smiling at me like that?"

"You're an angry little thing aren't you Charlie?" His question catches me off guard and I can't help but laugh. Who says that? I'm still laughing when he changes the subject.

"So, what brought you to Pleasant Grove at the end of your senior year? I'd be pissed at my parents for doing that shit to me." *Parents.* One of the few dreaded words that makes my mouth go dry and bile rise in my throat. Flashbacks of that night come rushing back to me.

The thunder crashes loudly outside of my pink colored room. I hold onto Mr. Snuggles as tightly as I can, but my stuffed bear isn't making me any less scared. I need mommy and daddy. Counting to three in my head I throw the covers off, jump up, and run straight to their bedroom door.

"Mommy! Daddy! I'm scared!" I cry as I try to jump onto their huge bed. Daddy helps me up as mommy turns on the light on her bedside table. They position me between the two of them and they each grab one of my hands.

"It's just thunder Char baby. You don't have anything to be scared of. We will always take care of you. Now, how about we play a game? " Daddy asks and I jump up and yell.

"The alphabet game, the alphabet game!"

Mommy laughs next to me and pulls me onto her lap. "Alright sweet girl, you go first," she says softly.

"I went to the supermarket and I got Apples," I say. "Your turn Daddy!"

"I went to the supermarket and I got apples and bunnies!" His answer makes me laugh hysterically.

"Daddyyyy why would you get bunnies at a super-"

CRASH!!! The sound of glass and wood breaking makes me scream and mommy hugs me tightly and whispers, "Shhhh."

"Jack, what was that?" Mommy whispers Daddy's real name, which means something's wrong.

"I don't know, I'm sure it's nothing, just stay up here and I'll be right back." Daddy gets up and grabs a golf club from inside his closet. He opens his bedroom door and slowly walks out into the hall-

way. That's when I hear their voices...

"Hello? Earth to Charlie? You still in there somewhere?" Paxton's voice breaks me out of my flashback and I take multiple deep breaths. The oxygen burns my lungs, proving I wasn't breathing during my flashback. "You okay? You zoned out for a while."

"Yeah... Um, I'm fine. Let's just go. We are going to be late for class." I start walking before he can stop me and luckily he doesn't push any farther. He simply walks next to me in silence until we reach our first class. Maybe he finally realized how weird I actually am.

CHAPTER 2

Paxton

I was in no mood when I showed up at school this morning. My father was driving me crazy about college. He kept saying I need to stop partying and playing sports and focus on my academics if I want to get into Harvard. I am in the top five percent of my graduating class...

And I don't necessarily want to go to an ivy league and follow in his footsteps...

When I made my way to the main office to find the idiot I had to show around, the last thing I expected to see was who I found. I walked slowly toward the girl slouching on the bench outside the office and watched as she laughed to herself. She looked a bit flustered, crazy even, and it brought a smile to my face for the first time all morning. I stood in front of her, waiting for her to notice me, and took in her appearance. Damn.

I'd never seen anyone quite like her in our small preppy town. She had shiny hair that cascaded down the sides of her face, completely hiding it from view. Instead of the perfectly styled and highlighted hair every girl in this damn school had, hers looked completely natural and a little messy. In a 'I just had sex' kind of way. Her body was covered in all black, but the dark clothes did nothing to hide her curves. Who was this creature?

I cleared my throat to get her attention, which seemed to startle her. Her eyes slowly made their way up my body until they were looking right into mine and holy shit. Her eyes were so blue they almost looked fake. Her face was covered in these adorable freckles. They covered her nose, her forehead, her cheeks, and went right down to her full lips that were parted just slightly. She was absolutely gorgeous.

Being the cocky prick I am, I made a stupid comment about her liking what she saw and it went downhill from there. She definitely isn't a fan of me but I am determined to change that. She feels like a breath of fresh air with her shy, hard to get, somewhat angry personality in this perfect, preppy, fake world I live in. I'm so used to every girl throwing themselves at me, so having Charlie physically running from me has me chasing after her without even knowing her last name yet.

CHAPTER 3

Charlie

The rest of the day goes by in a blur of confusing assignments and loud professors. Yes, they call the teachers here professors. Paxton got the hint after third period and stopped trying to make conversation with me... well, mostly. Every now and then he would crack some stupid joke to try to get me to laugh. I'll give it to him, he doesn't give up easily. People didn't notice me much, but I think it had more to do with the fact that everyone is obsessed with Paxton. He is clearly the most popular guy in this place. The amount of girls that were practically drooling over him was pretty pathetic. But he didn't seem to notice, or maybe he just didn't care. He seemed more concerned with school work, sports, and his friends. Oh, and of course, me. But I had a feeling that would change tomorrow since he was only with me so he didn't get in trouble with the school for ditching the new girl.

When the last bell rings, I grab my backpack, turn to Paxton, thank him for helping me, and book it out of the school. I hear Paxton yell my name but I don't stop. I just want to go home, curl up with a good book, and forget this weird day. I never had an issue staying in the shadows in my old schools. If someone tried to talk to me, they got the hint after my very uninterested attitude and left me alone. I know I seemed bitchy, but I have no reason to talk to anyone but my uncle. I don't trust people anymore, and for good reason. But Paxton seemed unaffected by my miserable attitude. I hate to admit it, but I actually started to enjoy his horrible jokes.

I decided to wander on my way back from school. The weather is perfect. Warm because of the bright sun, but still chilly with the breeze. With my headphones in, I walk along the windy road that leads to God knows where. The song 21 Guns invades my head and pushes everything else away. I watch the dark green pine trees sway in the cool breeze, their sappy needles dancing around each other from the wind. The smell of their strong pine scent hits my nose and instantly calms me. Closing my eyes I inhale deeply, appreciating this moment right here. The peaceful forest surrounding me. The music pumping into my ears. The road under my feet. Everything was perfect. Opening my eyes, I stare up at the blue sky for a few seconds before looking back at the road I was walking on. I look back down right in time to see a huge black truck coming right for me before screeching to a stop. The wheels skidded across the pavement, stopping less than two feet in front of me. Everything around me went blurry. The song faded into the background. My heart beat out of my chest. I stumble backwards, lost in the adrenaline that's surging through my body from my near death moment. I manage to trip on my own feet and end up on my back.

Everything happens in slow motion as a man jumps out of the truck and comes over to me, kneeling down next to me. His mouth is moving but I can't hear him, partly because I have headphones in but mostly because I'm in shock. I blink up at him and finally he starts to come into view. And that's when I see the darkest blue eyes I've ever seen in my life. Dark like the deepest depths of the ocean, swallowing you in a sea of water that you can never escape from. Those dangerous blue eyes blink back at me with what could only be described as a look of angry concern. His thick black eyebrows are furrowed and his mouth is permanently frowning, even when he speaks. His face is beautifully mysterious. He has scars etched through his plump bottom lip and right eyebrow. I watch as he lifts his arm and pushes back the curly black hair that is falling into his eyes. His jawline is as sharp as a knife, even under the layer of scruff that covers it. I can't look away from him. He is possibly the most beautiful creature I have ever laid my eyes on. And something about the look in his eyes reminds me of... me?

Mystery guy starts to shake his head at me, before he quickly reaches out and plucks the ear bud out of my ear, bringing me back to reality.

"Were you trying to get yourself killed?" His voice is deeper than I expected. The gravely tone reaches me to my core and makes me shiver.

"I... I" The words don't come out. The man shakes his head at me again and curses under his breath. I hear the word crazy come out of his mouth and that's all it takes for me to gain my voice back. "Maybe you should watch where you drive that piece of shit. I was minding my own business on the side of the road." The words come out louder than I expected, and I blame my newfound confidence on the adrenaline.

Deep laughter hits my ears. "Side of the road, huh? Sweetheart, you were walking on the goddamn yellow lines. If I wasn't paying attention you would be road kill right now." He starts to stand back up and I can't help but stare at his huge frame. He could easily be seven feet tall, and I've never seen muscles like his in real life. Every inch of his toned arms are covered in intricate black designs. My fingertips itch to reach out and trace the lines up under his shirt. *Deep breaths Charlie... get it together.*

The man reaches out toward me, and after a moment of hesitation, I put my hand in his. His warm hand engulfs mine completely, making me feel miniscule. He lifts me up with one quick pull and the change in altitude makes me dizzy again, so I reach out for something to keep me from falling. That something happens to be one really hard chest covered in a black t-shirt that matches my own. He lets me hold onto him as I steady myself. I can't seem to pull myself away from him. His shallow breaths moving his chest under my hands, and the soft beat of his heart are almost hypnotizing. I find myself being pulled to him, slowly walking towards him until I'm only a few inches away. Every part of me wants to touch him, to be touched by him. His eyes are staring into mine with a look of curiosity. I swear I see desire circling in his irises, but I may have hit my head when I fell. I'm barely breathing as I stare up into his stormy eyes. I watch him lick his lips, and my own mouth goes dry. His fingers push my wild hair behind my ear, grazing it as he does. The touch sends a lightning bolt through my entire body making me gasp.

Suddenly a car drives by us, breaking my trance, and what I'm doing hits me like a brick wall in the face. *Charlie what the fuck? This stranger almost killed you. And he's a huge scary man... just like... 'him'. There's a reason you don't let people in, why you don't let them touch you.*

I pull away quickly and back up a few steps. Mystery guy's eyebrows are furrowed again, and he looks just as confused about what happened as I am. He runs his hands through his hair and takes a deep breath.

"Look, I'm sorry I almost hit you. Did you hurt yourself when you fell? Hit your head on the ground?"

"Um, no. I uh... I don't think so." My voice is shaky.

"Well I don't trust it. Let me give you a ride home, it's the least I can do."

Instead of answering I simply shake my head no.

"Sweetheart, I'm not letting you walk home after I almost hit you with my truck. My piece of shit truck apparently. Please, let me help you." He is trying to make his raspy voice sound calming which ends up being more distracting, so I almost miss the sarcasm with the truck comment.

I let a strained laugh escape my lips for less than a second.

G. L. STRONG

"I'm sorry I said that. I was in shock. It's a very beautiful truck. Anyway, I like to walk. But thank you for the offer."

His lips turn up into a smirk, and it may just be the hottest thing I've ever seen. "If you really want to walk, I am going to end up following you with my truck going two miles per hour to make sure you are okay. If someone sees that, there's a very good chance the cops will be called. You don't wanna see me getting hauled off simply because I wanted to ensure your well-being, do you?" He raises one of his eyebrows and waits for me to respond.

"Fine." The word surprises me more than him when it escapes from my lips. *Why did you just agree to let a complete stranger drive you home? Have you lost your mind?* The smile that spreads across his face makes me roll my eyes.

"By the way, I'm Grayson, but you can call me Gray." He puts his hand out for me to shake it. Instead of reaching for it I simply walk past him and grab the passenger door handle to his impressive Chevy Silverado. I look back at him as I hoist myself up onto the seat, with a lot of difficulty I might add, and see him shake his head with a grin before he walks toward the truck. He hops in, in one swift movement, and then looks over at me. I refuse to look at him, worried I'll get lost in his eyes again, but I can feel his gaze across my body as I stare out the windshield.

"You know, when someone offers you their name, the normal response is to tell them yours." His voice is filled with humor and it bugs me for some reason.

"I'm not exactly normal." Is the only response I give back.

"Oh, I'm aware." His comment should have sounded rude, but something in the way he said it makes my cheeks flame with heat. Or maybe it was the way his eyes were slowly dragging down my body. "Are you going to make me guess your name?" He paused for my answer, which didn't come. "Alright. You definitely look like a Deliliah. Maybe a Precious? Petunia? Oh, I know. It's Crystal isn't it?" He was clearly messing with me, and I hated that it made me burst out into a fit of laughter. Before respond-

16

ing, I try to contain myself and look at him seriously.

"How did you guess on the third try? My name's Petunia... nice to meet you." I put my hand out to shake his, waiting for him to react. The look of shock and guilt takes over his features.

"Oh, shit I'm so sorry. I wasn't actually trying to make fun of you. Petunia is a beautiful name, it fits you really well." He softly grabs my hand to shake it, clearly feeling awkward. I can't hold it in anymore, I burst out laughing. I throw my head back and laugh harder than I have in, well, years. I must look like a crazy person, I know it isn't even that funny.

"I'm sorry, I- I'm sorry." I try to talk through my laughter. "Do I really look like a Petunia to you?" I keep on laughing, while he sits there staring at me like I have lost my mind. *Maybe I finally have.* Once I can breathe again, I look over at him. That's when I realize our hands are still intertwined between us. "Um... my uh. My name is Charlie."

"Charlie, huh?" I wait for him to make a comment about it being a guy's name. "Now that's a beautiful name." As he says it, he squeezes my hand a little tighter and his thumb brushes up and down against my skin, making tingles shoot up my arm. The feeling is too intense and I pull away, turning to look out the window again. His low chuckle hits my ears again before he adds. "But, I think I like Petunia better."

I can't tell if he is joking about the name Petunia or about the person that came out of me when I was pretending to be her. Either way, the sarcastic, playful comment chips at the small amount of confidence I'm radiating. I close my eyes and see myself on my eyelids again. Big smile, shiny hair cascading down my back, a yellow sundress tight around my chest but falling loose down to my mid-thigh. She looks like a Petunia. A soft, sweet, girl who simply smiled and the world fell at her feet. She would fit in with all of the perfect girls at Pleasant Grove. She would have been the center of attention today, and she would have loved it. Petunia starts spinning on my eyelids and her bubbly laugh echoes through my mind. She spins and spins, surrounded by complete darkness and not caring. The darkness shifts and behind the spinning girl, a figure slowly comes into view. And then another. Their frames were intimidatingly large. They wore the same black sweatshirts I always saw them in with the hoods up, making it hard to see any features on their faces. But I know who they are. I can make out their sinister smiles as they walk up to Petunia, who is completely oblivious. Their dark eyes pierce her skin, watching her every move with hunger. I want to scream at her, to tell her to watch out, but I know it wouldn't help. Screaming never did. It only made things worse. I watch as they finally reach her and each one of them grips her upper arms hard enough to leave bruises. Petunia's face changes instantly, from a genuine smile, to a look of dread and fear. A look of no hope. Of nothingness. Her eyes go dull and she crumples into herself. The sight makes me wince, as I will myself to open my eyes. Instead, they remain closed and I watch as they kick her feet out from under her and drag her backwards with them, into the darkness. My eyes stay shut until the girl before me is gone and all I can hear is their sinister laughter. They are the reason Petunia doesn't exist.

CHAPTER 4

Gray

I hate him. That stupid smug grin on his lips plays over and over in my mind as I drive down the windy roads of town. He knows he owns me. Knows I have no power in any of this shit. He's the puppet master and when he yanks on those fucking strings, I have no choice but to go with the motions. His words repeat in my mind as I white knuckle the steering wheel.

"You know what will happen if you disobey me Grayson. One call and Ava is gone. You'll never see her again and you can't imagine the things she'll endure." His words scared the shit out of me because I knew how true they were. He owned this town. Owned this state. Fuck, he was close with every important person in this country and closer with every criminal. He had law enforcement under his thumb. I know this because I tried to go to the cops when I turned eighteen, three years ago, and I am the one that ended up in jail. I had the evidence. I have been working for the man since I was fourteen. I knew about the drug cartel, the sex trafficking, the shady deals he made with political figures. He put on a great show of being the small town mayor who loved his family and worked hard. But he was a monster. And I wanted him dead.

Dead… Dead… Dead. The word is on repeat in my brain. Getting louder and louder, matching my racing heart as I picture the man, who has owned me since I was just a boy, lifeless. An extremely windy turn comes up and I know I'm going too fast. I start to slow down when I spot a girl walking in the middle of the road, looking up at the sky and I slam on my brakes when I see she isn't going to move. Screeching comes from my tires as my truck swerves from side to side until it finally comes to a stop right in front of the biggest blue eyes I have ever seen. She looks like a deer in the headlights, staring straight ahead at the front of my Chevy. I see the fear and shock radiating from her eyes, but there is something else there too... something that resembles emptiness. The feeling I know all too well. I hop out of my truck and run to her when I see her fall to the ground and come face to face with the most beautiful sadness I have ever seen in my life.

And now that beautiful, sad girl is sitting in my passenger seat as I pull up to a small house in the shitty part of town, not too far from my own apartment. I look over at her as I put my truck in park on the side of the road. Her steel blue eyes are glued to my windshield. Her button nose curves down to a pair of the softest looking lips I have ever seen. They are the lightest pink color, something that shouldn't be natural, but I know it is. She doesn't have a lick of makeup on, apparent by the maze of freckles all over her face. Her dark brown hair falls long down her back in messy waves. I let my eyes wander down her body and can't control how my own reacts to the sight. She's wearing a simple outfit of black jeans and a shirt, but they don't hide the curves under them. She's effortlessly gorgeous and I can't stop staring at her. But that feeling clearly isn't mutual. Charlie has barely looked my way since I tried to joke with her about her name. Something in her face changed and she disappeared into herself, only providing one word directions until we reached her house. I tried to apologize, but I swear it's like she didn't even hear it. I can tell this girl has some demons, and all I want to do is push her behind me and growl at any evil that tries to get to her. Like a damn dog. Fuck me.

"Look, I'm sorry if we got off on the wrong foot. I didn't mean to offend you. I actually live a few blocks down so I'm sure we will be seeing more of each other." I don't know why I care so much about this girl liking me, but I can't seem to stop the words from coming out of my mouth. "If you ever need a ride, or just need someone to stare up at the sky with, here's my number." I grab a crumpled up napkin and try to make my number as clear as possible, handing it over to Charlie. She hesitates before finally looking my way, but doesn't reach for the napkin.

"Sweetheart, It's just a piece of paper. If you don't want it you can just throw it away and forget you ever met me."

"Well, um, it may be hard to forget the guy who uh almost ran me over." The words come out awkward, like she forgot how to tell a joke, and dear Lord it's cute. I can't contain my smile as I stare at her, and when the sides of her lips curve up just slightly, I damn near almost grab her face and kiss her right there.

Instead, she grabs the napkin out of my hand, opens the door, and practically falls out of my truck, before turning around and looking back up at me. "Thanks for bringing me home, Gray." My name on her lips is barely a whisper but it's enough to make my body react.

"Anytime sweetheart. Be careful walking on these roads... there are a bunch of assholes in this town that drive too fast." I wink at her and she smirks back at me before giving me an awkward wave and closing her door. I'd be lying if I said I didn't watch her walk to the house. To make sure she was safe, not to watch her ass bounce as she sped up the unmanicured lawn, obviously.

My phone starts ringing, bringing me back to my shitty reality. Picking up my cell from my center console, I see the puppet master's name across the top of my screen. I know if I ignore him there will be hell to pay, so begrudgingly, I pick up.

"Why the fuck are you across town and not driving to the drop off spot?" His voice is like nails on a chalkboard.

"Tracking me again I see. I'm headed there now." My voice is short and clipped, like it always is with him.

"If you don't stop jerking off and get that package to Santiago in the next hour, there will be hell to pay." I hear a door open and close on the other side of the phone. "Speaking of who will pay," he whispers into the phone before yelling. "Hi Ava darling, how was school today?" Bile rises in my throat every time I hear him say her name. I can barely hear her sweet voice responding through the phone.

"That's wonderful darling. What do you say you and I go out to dinner tonight? That is, if Grayson isn't home before then. If he is, maybe he can come with us. The reservation is at 5:30." I hear the threat in his words and my blood starts to boil. I don't hear Ava's response, but he tells her to go put on her prettiest dress.

"Be a shame if you weren't here in time, Grayson. I have someone who wants to meet her and it just so happens he will be at the same restaurant we are going to. The clock is ticking."

"You son of a-" The call goes out before I can finish the sentence. "FUCK!" I can't help but scream as I hit the steering wheel. I look at the clock, 3:45. That means I have less than 2 hours to get to the drop off spot, which is an hour away, and then make it back to his house. I put the truck in drive and press the gas to the floor, counting down the minutes until I can get to Ava.

CHAPTER 5

Charlie

Slamming the front door behind me I finally take a moment to breathe. What the hell just happened? First Paxton, and now Grayson. I look down at the napkin in my hand and consider what to do with it. Making my way over to the garbage can I press the button with my foot and the top lifts open. The napkin feels heavy in my hand as I reach out over the trash to throw it away. Only, I can't do it. My hand won't open up, no matter how much I try to. Huffing, I step off the button and walk over to the kitchen counter. Unfolding the napkin, I look at the numbers sprawled across the paper. *It won't hurt to have someone's number in town.* My mind is desperately trying to convince me to program his number into my phone. Before I know what I'm doing, my phone is out and his name is added to my contact list. Looking down at the name, my finger hovers over the message button. Every part of me wants to talk to him again and that scares the crap out of me. I never want to talk to anyone. My phone buzzes in my hand making me jump and throw it to the counter. I grab my chest and feel my heart racing under my hand.

Jesus Charlie... get it together!

I grab my phone and open up my messages. Part of me wishes it was Grayson's name in my inbox, but I remind myself that he doesn't have my number. Instead, Uncle Brian's name pops up. His message is just letting me know there is food in the fridge for dinner and not to wait up. He always sends the same message when he starts his work shift. Sending back a thumbs up, I make my way over to the fridge. My uncle stocked the fridge at some point between this morning and now, which I am grateful for.

Grabbing ingredients for chicken parm, I close the fridge and start cooking. I watched my mom cook when I was little, and it's something I like to do now to make myself feel closer to her. When I smash the garlic, I see her teaching me to put all of my weight down on the knife. I hear her laugh when I throw the pasta at the wall to see if it's cooked. She only did that as a joke when I was younger, but I have been doing it ever since. She taught me how to cook, and no one can take those memories away from me. I continue chopping and slicing with a smile on my face as I think about my mom. The aroma of sizzling garlic and fresh tomato sauce fills the room. I finally put the chicken in the oven and decide to go get some homework done. Retracing my steps, I look for my backpack, coming up short. The realization hits me. I was so distracted with my heart beating out of my chest and Grayson's eyes staring at me that I left it in his truck.

"Shitttt." The word hangs in the air as I think of what to do. I know the easy answer is to just message him, but my mind seems to skip right past that idea and move to more logical things like search the internet for new textbooks that would obviously get here in the next few hours.

Screw it, one day of not having my homework done won't kill me. Now I can read instead and figure out the textbook and backpack debacle tomorrow. I grab one of the many books off the bookshelf Uncle Brian made for me and sit down at the dining room table. I open it up and start inhaling each word. The story is about a girl who falls in love with her brother's best friend. I eat these stories up like they are candy. They are my absolute favorite type of book, which is ironic, since I have never been in love with anyone.

Forty-five minutes later the food is ready and I'm scarfing down a plate. Once I'm finished, I wash the dishes and find myself lying on the couch, full to the brim. The warm, comforting haze of being so full takes over my body and my eyelids start to get heavy. I grab the blanket off the back of the couch and decide a nap is just what I need.

"Wake up little one." I can feel daddy's hand on my arm, shaking me awake. I toss around in my sleep and try to pull away, I'm just so tired. The shaking becomes more violent then, and the grip on my arm tightens making me cry out.

"Daddy that hurts." I am holding back tears as I open my eyes and look up to see why Daddy is holding me so tight. Only, I can't see daddy with his black hood over his head. It's too dark in the room to make anything out except his body standing over me.

"You can call me daddy." A gruff voice answers me and my body freezes from fright.

The man laughs darkly. That's not daddy...

The scary man is still holding onto my arm and then he rips me up so I'm standing. The scream that escapes me echoes through the room. That's when I hear another laugh coming from the darkness and I want to close my eyes and pretend I'm not here.

"Turn on the lights." The voice in the darkness speaks up. Suddenly, my eyes are blinded by light and I cry out from the pain, trying to hide my poor eyeballs in my hands. Scary man doesn't let me though, he grabs onto my other arm and stands behind me, pulling my arms back with him so I can't move.

I look around the room with my burning eyeballs, noticing the dirty bed I was sleeping on, the little toilet next to it, and a big man sitting in the corner with his hood on too. Why would someone put a toilet next to their bed? That's yucky.

I see movement coming from the man in the corner and watch as he reaches up and removes his hood. He has no hair on his head which looks silly. Where did his hair go? His eyes are staring right at me. They are so black that they look like two cups of Daddy's gross coffee on his face. He's so big. I think he's the biggest person on this planet. I watch as a smile appears on his face, but it doesn't make me want to smile back. It makes me want to cry and turn away.

"You're such a pretty girl, Charlotte. Boss was right, you're going to make us lots of money." His comment confuses me. I'm only seven, how can I make them money? Yeah, I'll be eight soon, but I only have 23 dollars in my piggy bank.

"How long until Antonio is ready for her?" The man holding me asks. Antonio is a pretty name.

"He doesn't want her until he is ready to leave the country next month. He wants us to drop her at the landing pad the minute before he takes off." I've never been on a plane! I would be more excited if it wasn't with these people. Maybe they know where my mommy and daddy went. Maybe they will be on the plane!

"Mmmhh so we get you for a whole month?" The scary guy behind me says that in my ear and I try to pull away. I don't like when people whisper in my ear.

"Can't you bring me to my Mommy? Please? I'll be really good. Mommy and Daddy always tell me I'm a good girl. I say please and thank you and I do my chores and I share my toys with kids in school. Please?" I'm begging them, trying to convince them that I am a good girl. I think maybe I convinced them, until they both start laughing at me. It makes me cry because it's not nice to laugh at people.

"Oh little one, I'm sure you'll be a really good girl." The scary man behind me says while he rubs my arms. I look at the man in the corner as he watches us both.

"Where's mommy and daddy? I miss them, please?" I'm bawling as I look at the hairless man in the corner, begging him to bring mommy and daddy.

The man starts to stand up and walk over to me. I try to back away but the other man is behind me and won't let me move. He *comes over to me and kneels down so his gross face is near mine. He reaches a hand out and pushes the hair out of my face, tucking it behind my ear. He looks into my eyes before he says the worst thing I have ever heard in my life. "Your mommy and daddy are dead."*

I wake up hearing the screams of seven year old me echoing through my head. I wish it was just a nightmare. I wish it was all fake. Just something my mind created after watching too many scary movies. But, it's not fake. It's a memory that holds me hostage, one of many. I can still feel his slimy hands on my arms and the way their eyes looked at my tiny body. I needed to shower.

I grab my phone off the coffee table and look at the time, 8:45 pm. Getting up, I head over to the bathroom upstairs. Stripping from my clothes, I turn the water on. Right when I step under the steaming hot water, I hear the doorbell ring. I wait a few seconds before moving, waiting to see if it rings again. It does, and I roll my eyes. It's probably Uncle Brian, coming home early because he got too drunk at work and they sent him home. He forgets his key way too often. I grab the white towel I set out for myself and quickly fold it around my now wet body.

Running down the stairs, the doorbell rings again, and I huff at his impatience.

I reach the door, and as I open it I say, "I know you can't help but get drunk on the job, but could you at least remember your ke-" My words are cut off when I look into his blue eyes. Grayson is standing on my front porch, smirk and all. He's about to say something, until he realizes what I'm wearing. His eyes wander down my barely covered body, and heat flames in his eyes. We stand there in silence, him staring at me and me frozen where I stand. I'm horrified. I can feel my cheeks are blazing red, and I pull the towel tighter to my body.

"Um... sorry, I uh, didn't realize it was you." I look down at my towel. "Obviously."

He laughs and runs his hands through his hair, still looking at my body. At this point I'm pretty sure my face is bright red.

Finally, he manages to peel his eyes off my towel, and looks me right in the eyes. Which isn't much better, since I can see the desire swirling in them. "Um, sorry Charlie. I wasn't thinking before I showed up. It didn't cross my mind that I could be, um, interrupting something." He was stumbling on his words, something I'm very used to, and the sight made me smile.

"I was just about to take a shower. I'm sorry, I thought you were my uncle so I didn't think twice about answering the door like this."

"You walk around like this in front of your uncle?" His tone changed and he looked a little angry. I realize that probably didn't sound the best to someone else.

"It's not like that, he's not really just my uncle. I live with him, I have since I was little. He's my legal guardian. I'm like a daughter to him so he's seen me in a towel before. Hell, he helped bathe me when I was a little girl, he's seen more of me than any-" *Oh my god. What am I saying? I'm word vomiting all over him about my uncle seeing me naked as a little girl... And did I just admit that no one else has ever seen me naked? Well, not nobody. No. Stop. Don't think of them right now. Jesus Charlie. Real classy.* "Um. Anyway, I'm going to stop talking now."

"You're really cute Charlie, did you know that?" He was laughing at me again. He tends to do that a lot.

"Um, why are you here?" It sounds rude when it comes out of my mouth, but it's a valid question.

"Shit, right. I'm here for a reason." He reaches down and grabs my backpack, which I hadn't noticed. "You left this in my truck. I was going to bring it earlier but I uh, had some time sensitive errands to run." I notice the flash of anger in his eyes before he smiles at me again. "I didn't realize you were still in school. And a part of me feels really guilty for liking the way you look right now because I have no idea how old you are." His comment makes goosebumps spread across my arms.

"I'm seventeen, I'll be eighteen next week. Thank you for

bringing my bag back." I wonder why I felt the need to clarify that I was almost eighteen. It's not like I have interest in talking to him like that. No, none at all.

"Oh, thank god. Now I can look and not feel too guilty." He was joking around with me, but his eyes did slowly make their way down and back up. It takes me a second to realize that if he was worried about me being under eighteen, he was clearly older. My curiosity gets the best of me.

"Um, so how old are you?" I ask nervously while I grip my towel tightly.

"I just turned twenty-one. Don't worry, I'm not that much older than you, sweetheart." His stupid smirk is back.

"I'm not worried. I was just curious," I replied defensively.

"Oh yeah?" He steps in closer. "So you weren't asking because you were worried that I was some creepy older guy checking you out? Or maybe you were worried because you like how it feels when my eyes are all over your almost naked body? Is that why you asked Charlie?" His voice was husky and filled with desire.

I swallow hard and will my heart to shut up. It was hammering in my ears, and I was sure he could hear it. My whole body was humming with something I've never experienced before.

"I, uh. I." The words wouldn't come out. Gray looks down at me, stepping closer again.

He keeps his eyes on mine the entire time. My chest is rising and falling, begging for more air. But there isn't enough oxygen in this world to calm my frantic breaths.

I watch as his hand reaches toward me ever so slowly. His warm fingertips brush from my neck down to my collarbone, stealing my breath and making me gasp. A deep growl fills my ears and it's the most amazing sound I've ever heard. He pulls his hand away and wipes his fingers on his pants, which confuses me.

"You had a few drops of water dripping down that pretty little neck of yours, sweetheart." His explanation is barely a whisper. He swallows hard and I watch as his eyes move from my eyes to my lips. He licks his own and a shiver runs through my body. That seems to catch his attention, and his brows furrow slightly.

"Shit, you must be freezing, it's cold out tonight and you are pretty much naked." Ugh. He needs to stop saying the word naked. "I'm sorry I kept you out here so long, why don't you finish up that shower and maybe I can see you again soon?" His question catches me off guard since my body is still humming with desire. Instead of thinking, I simply nod my head yes.

"Great, how about tomorrow night? I'll pick you up at 6. Now, go get in that shower and warm up before I lose all sense of control and haul you up there myself to join you." His comment makes me gasp again and he shakes his head with a strained laugh. "If you gasp like that one more time, I may not be able to convince myself to leave Charlie. Get your sweet ass inside, I'll see you tomorrow." With that, he turns around and walks back to his truck.

What just happened?

Did I just agree to a date with Gray?

I'm still standing in the cold entry way, staring at Gray's truck as it roars to life. I watch his window roll down before I see his face again.

"Do me a favor and lock your door. And don't answer it in a towel unless you know it's me. Good night, sweetheart."

His truck starts to pull away and I wait until all I can hear are the crickets chirping in the night. That's when I'm able to breathe. I turn around quickly and slam the door shut, locking it in the process. I replay everything that just happened. Gray showing up at my door. The way he made me feel by just looking at me. No one has ever made me feel that way. I have always been embarrassed by my body. I've always wished my arms were thinner. That my belly was perfectly flat and my thighs didn't rub together when I walked. And don't get me started on the scars.

The scars that no one ever saw. The scars that dug into my back, my stomach, my hips.

They put them there. Making sure I could never forget them. They made me ugly...

But Gray made me feel beautiful. He made me feel wanted, made me want something I have never wanted before. I barely knew this man, but I could almost hear the walls around me slowly starting to crack every time he looked at me or called me sweetheart.

I made my way upstairs and got in the shower. Letting the scalding hot water wash away all thoughts of my nightmare and the feelings Gray was bringing out of me. After fifteen minutes I got out and went into my room to put on pajamas. I noticed a uniform folded up on top of my bed with a note on top of it.

This was in the mailbox. Bet your day started off pretty shitty being the only one at school without a uniform... sorry kid. Can't wait to hear about your first day. Love, Brian.

I shook my head at the note, thankful that I now had a uniform to wear tomorrow. The clock on my nightstand read 9:45 and I sigh at the thought of doing homework at this hour. I almost wish Gray hadn't shown up tonight so I didn't have to do any of it... almost.

Putting on an oversized t-shirt and a pair of boy shorts, I grab my backpack and get to work on the stack of homework in front of me.

CHAPTER 6

Charlie

I wake up the next morning feeling oddly refreshed. My body doesn't feel sore, my eyes don't feel bloodshot, and my mind is clear. I sit up wondering why and then realize I don't remember having a single nightmare last night. Every night for the last ten years I have had at least one nightmare about my time with them. What changed? My mind whispers the word *Gray*, but I force it down and ignore it.

Changing into my uniform, I look at myself in the mirror. The white button up is a bit wrinkly, and I have the sleeves rolled up halfway. The shirt is tucked into a burgundy plaid skirt, which reaches about mid-thigh. I have my doc martens on, since they are the only shoes I ever wear. In my hand I hold the matching tie that I'm supposed to know how to put on. I try to tie it, and after three failed attempts, I give up and throw the tie in my backpack. Running my hands through my tangled wavy hair, I decide to try something different and put my hair up. I manage to get most of it into the high ponytail, but a few tendrils escape around my face. That's as good as it's gonna get, I sigh before I sling my backpack over my shoulder and head out the door.

The walk to school is uneventful, which I am extremely grateful for. I make my way into the large building, arriving ten minutes early, and head for the designated locker that Paxton helped me find yesterday. I keep my head down, and avoid eye contact with anyone passing by. It's a force of habit at this point.

Reading the numbers on each locker I continue down the hall until I reach locker number 263. Only, when I get there, there's a very large body blocking my view of it. He is standing with his back to me talking to someone, so I let my eyes wander down from his messy brown hair, to his tight slacks that do a terrible job at hiding what's underneath. Once I reach the locker, I can see who Paxton is talking to. A petite girl with shiny blonde hair, bright blue eyes, and, oh yeah, boobs that are practically spilling out of her unbuttoned top. She is laughing at something Paxton said, and she reaches out and hits his arm playfully telling him to *"oh my gosh, stop that right now!"* In the squeakiest voice I have ever heard. The sound makes me cringe as I stand there and wait patiently for them to stop talking and move. Her eyes finally look my way and a look of disgust covers her perfect little face.

"Can I help you, new girl? We are kind of in the middle of something." Instead of answering I just shake my head no and look down, wanting more than anything to avoid the mean girl attitude she is projecting my way. I hear her mumble the word freak under her breath and I try not to let it get to me. I've been called worse. Before I can turn around and walk away Paxton speaks up.

"Charlie! I've been waiting for you." He reaches out for me and hooks an arm into mine. The movement is quick enough that I don't have time to react. "See ya, Brooke." He doesn't notice the look of shock on her face as he smiles down at me. I hear Brooke whine "Paxyyy" before she huffs and turns around, swaying her hips as she speed walks away from us.

"You just put a target on my back, Paxton. I don't talk to people for a reason. And now she hates me and I haven't even said a word to her." I pull away from him and reach for the combination on my locker. I hear the sound of my backpack unzipping and turn my head to see Paxton behind me, grabbing my chemistry book out of my bag.

"She doesn't hate you. She's just jealous she doesn't look as hot as you do in the school uniform. Did I mention you look great in a skirt?" His joke makes me laugh. Like anyone would ever look at me and Brooke and decide I was the hotter one. That's a good one.

"Ha Ha. You're so funny," I say as I throw my backpack into my locker and grab the textbook out of Paxton's hands. "She is pissed that you stopped talking to her to talk to me. She clearly wants you, just like every other girl in this place."

"Every other girl, huh?" He is leaning against the other lockers now, staring right at me.

"Pretty much. I'm not exactly a social person. Which gives me ample time to watch everyone around me. I've gotten pretty good at reading people."

"Not that good, clearly." Paxton says it under his breath and I almost miss it.

"What?" His comment makes me self-conscious about what I said. Why did I just admit that? Why am I still talking to him? "Never mind, sorry. I don't know why I said that. You should go talk to Brooke. I have to get to class." I close my locker and turn away from him, hoping he just leaves me alone.

"Charlie girl, don't shut down on me now. I was just starting to get some actual sentences out of you!" Of course he wouldn't just leave me alone. His comment makes me roll my eyes. "Don't you roll your eyes at me, miss. I took the time out of my day to help you find your way yesterday, all out of the kindness of my heart." He puts his hand to his chest and pretends to sniffle.

Laughing at his dramatics, I look up at him with a raised eyebrow. "Oh really? Kindness of your heart? So it had nothing to do with staying on good terms with the school administration?"

"How dare you accuse me of such a thing! I should bend you

over my knee and spank you with the wooden paddle in Mrs. Burgs office for starting rumors like that." His voice was full of humor, but when I looked up at his eyes I saw him admiring my body in a way that almost resembled how Gray did last night. *Jesus, this is too much.*

I simply shake my head at Paxton with a laugh, refusing to feed into his theatrics. Of course, that doesn't stop him.

"You know, technically you owe me one now, Charlie girl." He is smiling at me as we approach the chemistry room. Before I can enter, he pulls me to the side of the door and looks down at me. "Seriously, you owe me one." His voice is low and I can't help the chill that runs through my body. The way he says that almost sounds threatening, but looking at the genuine smile on his face, I know it was just a joke.

"I owe you one for driving me crazy all day yesterday? That doesn't exactly seem fair." The comment makes him chuckle lightly as he looks into my eyes.

"Fine. Then I owe you one for annoying the shit out of you. Why don't you let me drive you home from school? I noticed you walking when you left yesterday and it wouldn't feel right letting you do that when I have an extremely comfortable, warm passenger seat in my car. I was raised to be a gentleman Charlotte."

"I really like walking though." The look in his eyes could only be compared to a sad puppy. Good Lord. "Alright. Fine. You can drive me home from school if it means you'll stop looking at me like that." I don't bother to wait for his answer, I walk into the room and ignore him the rest of class.

***

I'm realizing there is favoritism in this stupid school. Walking around, I can spot at least ten preppy perfect little girls with no ties, and their shirts barely buttoned. But, I walk around with my shirt buttoned up to my neck, minus a tie, and it's a damn sin. I had been scolded by 4 of my professors for not wearing my tie by the end of the day. I didn't try to explain that I have no idea how to put it on, I simply nodded my head and said sorry ma'am or sir. As much as the professors didn't seem to like me, I actually enjoy most of my classes. Chemistry is a bit boring, mostly because the teacher talks way too much, but the rest of my classes are great. I have English Lit second period, which is my favorite since all we have to do is read classic romance novels like *The Great Gatsby* and *Wuthering Heights.* Professor Kate gave us a syllabus with all of the books we will be reading this year, and I read through it late last night. I have to admit, I am beyond excited to start reading *Sense and Sensibility* by Jane Austen. After English, I had Statistics, Physics, and then lunch. Lunch is a real treat. Paxton tried to get me to sit with him at a table full of intimidating guys, but I opted for a more comfortable spot. The huge library, which is located at the opposite end of the school. It had three different levels, with books filed all the way up from floor to ceiling. It's by far my favorite part of this school. Lastly, I had Ceramics and then Gym class. Gym is the worst part of the day. We had to change into gym clothes, which in my opinion are highly inappropriate to be wearing in school. The girls out-fits consist of a tight maroon t-shirt and matching bottoms that would be best described as small biker shorts, completely form fitting. They both sport the school's letters, PG, in white font. *Oh, the irony.* We played field hockey, splitting off into two different games, one with guys and one with girls. Of course, I was picked last when the girls were picking teams.

Now, I'm sitting outside the school, waiting for Paxton to drive me home. I spot him walking out with three other guys. They look like your typical arrogant jocks. When Paxton spots me, he gives me a big smile and then I watch as he says something to the three guys surrounding him. All three of their heads turn my way when he speaks, and it's obvious he is talking about me. My cheeks blush at the sudden attention and I want to hit Paxton in his handsome face for constantly making people see me. I watch as all four of them start laughing hysterically and I turn away in shame. They are probably talking about how big my thighs look in this skirt. Or how small my boobs are compared to all the other girls at this school. Or how I look like a guy with my hair up like this. That last one gets to me and I grip the hair tie with my hand and let my dull, sweaty locks fall over my shoulders. I don't dare glance back at the guys, knowing it will only make me feel more self-conscious.

"Hey hot stuff." The comment comes from one of the guys with Paxton when they pass by. It makes me sick to my stomach, knowing he is just making fun of me. I watch as Paxton punches him in the arm and says his goodbyes.

"You ready Charlie girl?" He puts his hand out for me to take, since I'm sitting on one of the stonewalls that adorn the school's entryway. I sigh heavily and put my hand in his, letting him help me up. "What's wrong? I'm sorry if John made you uncomfortable. He doesn't have a filter."

"It's fine, I'm used to being made fun of. It doesn't bother me anymore," I say genuinely and give him a small smile. I'm greeted by a look of confusion in Paxton's eyes.

"Making fun of you? I'm sorry, now I'm lost."

"Paxton. I'm not stupid. I know when someone is making fun of me. 'Hot stuff' isn't usually the nickname people choose for me." I huff, annoyed at myself for even bringing it up.

"Oh Charlie, you are so damn wrong. You are the definition of hot stuff. Your huge eyes that constantly look so sad. Those lips of yours." He reaches out and grazes my bottom lip with his thumb. Paxton groans. "Those lips that are as soft as they look. Your legs in that skirt today were unbelievably distracting to not just me, but every other student and professor in this place. I don't know where you came from, but whoever made you think you were anything shy of gorgeous is clearly blind." His confession makes me speechless.

I have always lived in the shadows. People didn't notice me because I didn't want them to. I purposely covered my body and didn't wear any makeup to prevent anyone from looking twice. His confession made me happy, but it also scared the shit out of me. I didn't want to be distracting to people. I wanted to hide in the background where no one could find me. Where *they* couldn't find me.

"Anyway, how about we get going before I embarrass myself even more?" Paxton must clearly feel uncomfortable after his confession. Especially since I didn't say anything back to him. It made me feel a bit guilty. He was so genuinely nice to me, and I needed to stop being so bitchy and worried around him.

Before I can stop myself, I get on my tippy toes and give Paxton a hug. He doesn't react at first, but suddenly he wraps his arms around me and hugs me back. My heart starts to race at the feeling of a huge frame holding onto me, but I will my brain not to go there. "Thank you Paxton, for everything." I give him another quick squeeze and then pull away.

"You Charlie girl, are going to be the death of me." His words come out a bit huskier than they were before our hug as I watch him adjust his pants. The sight makes me blush and I decide to take that moment to walk ahead of him into the parking lot. He finally catches up to me and leads me to a silver Porsche. The car lights up when he presses the key and I stop in my tracks.

"*That* is your car?" I let my mouth hang open as I look at it in awe.

"Yeah, it's not the model I wanted but she does the job." I laugh at his joke, until I realize he isn't joking. I open up the passenger door and carefully get into the expensive piece of machinery. I keep my hands on my lap, in fear of getting the interior dirty with my lower class hands.

"Are you like a celebrity or something?" I mean to say that in my head but the words just fly out of my mouth. "Sorry, I wasn't trying to be rude."

Paxton laughs. "Don't be sorry, and kind of actually. My dad is Mayor Whitlock."

"So I'm friends with the mayor's son? Wow, guess I'm pretty much a celebrity now too."

I feel so comfortable joking with him, it's a nice change.

"Friends, huh? I'm torn. Half of me loves that you consider us friends already. But the other half hates the word and never wants you to refer to me as a friend again." It takes me almost thirty seconds to realize what he means, but when I do, I start laughing.

"What, never been friend-zoned?"

"Are you saying I am being friend-zoned?" he asks me seriously this time as he puts his car into drive and we move forward.

I don't quite know how to respond. I like Paxton, he's handsome and sweet, but I have never been in a relationship with anyone before. I've never willingly kissed someone. I don't know the first thing about dating. Besides that, I have a date tonight with another man. Another man that I just met. Who saw me in a towel less than 24 hours ago and who made my body feel things it's never felt before. *I'm so screwed.* I realize it's been a good two minutes since he asked me that question and sigh when I know I have to answer.

"Um, I really don't know, Paxton. This is all new to me and we just met yesterday. We barely know each other. I've never dated anyone before so I don't know what I want, mostly because I've never had it." The confession hits me hard as I hear the words come out of my mouth. How pathetic do I sound? I'm almost eighteen years old and I've never experienced love or anything close to it. I've never been on a date, never had an awkward first kiss, never been touched by someone I care about. No one has ever told me they were in love with me... no one has ever told me they liked me... well, until now. Those assholes stole so much from me, and I never realized what hiding myself away from the rest of the world was doing... It was letting them win.

"I get it, Charlie. I'm not saying we should date, I know we just met and I wouldn't expect that. I just want to get to know you, like really get to know you. All I know so far is you are gorgeous, smart, hotheaded, a little fucking scary sometimes, and different from anyone I have ever met. Maybe I like pain, but I enjoy spending time with you even when you treat me like shit." He laughed halfway through the last sentence, and I couldn't help but laugh with him.

"You're crazy Paxton Whitlock. You just met me yesterday."

"Well I've never met anyone like you and you're all I've been thinking about the last 24 hours. Now tell me how to get to your house, gorgeous."

The five minute drive to my house goes by too quickly and when Paxton pulls up to the curb outside of the small chalet home, I sit there trying to think of what to say to avoid getting out. Then it hits me.

"Can you help me with something?" The words spill out of my mouth.

"What's up?"

Instead of answering, I grab my backpack and start ruffling through it until my hand grasps the silky fabric and I pull out my tie. "I have no idea how to tie this thing... wanna show me?"

Paxton smiles from ear to ear. "God, you're so cute Charlie." The statement makes me blush. I realize I may never get used to his sweet talk.

I hand him the tie and let him take over. He grabs the fabric and reaches towards me to place it around my neck. We both have to lean into the center console in order for him to reach.

Once the tie is around my neck, I reach up and do a quick flip of my hair to get it out of the way.

I watch as Paxton's Adam's apple bobs up and down with his swallow. He is staring at my face, moving from my eyes to my lips, before he looks down at the tie in his hands. They start to move, delicately but fast, and I can't keep up with what he's doing. Before I know it the tie is fastened in a perfect knot, and he reaches for it with both hands before slowly pulling it until it's tight. His fingers brush against the skin on my neck. Instead of pulling them away, he lets his fingers linger there and then brushes them up until they reach my jawline. That somewhat familiar hum returns, but it's very faint. His hand cups the side of my face and his thumb brushes up against my cheek.

"You're so beautiful." The words are sweet to my ears, but they make me nervous. I know he wants to kiss me right now, I'm not that naive. Part of me wants to know what it would feel like. But the other part of me worries it will bring out flashbacks that I desperately don't want to remember.

I don't have time to think much further into it before Paxton bends forward in one swift movement and captures my lips with his. It takes me by surprise and I feel like I'm in shock at first. I don't know what to do, how to move, nothing. But, then he moves his lips on mine and something changes. His soft lips spark an electricity in my body that surprises me. I close my eyes and let myself get lost in the kiss, in the touch of his hands on my face. My lips start to move on their own accord and the hum in my body intensifies. Suddenly, I feel a warm wet heat on my lower lip and realize it's Paxton's tongue. The feeling makes me gasp and then Paxton's tongue invades my mouth. His hand on my cheek is still gentle, but his mouth starts to devour my own. I try to keep up with his kiss, feeling unsure, until I hear a growl from Paxton's throat and his grip on my face gets tighter. He is pulling me towards him, grabbing onto me to get better leverage.

A sharp pain engulfs my bottom lip and makes me wince. It takes me a second to realize that he bit me, and by that time, he is sucking the same spot which dulls the pain. Suddenly I feel overwhelmed and when my eyes close I see *their* faces. I see the hairless man walking up to me on my bed. I feel his hands on my neck as he squeezes just enough until I am gasping for air. I feel his filthy mouth kiss its way across my face, the painful bite to my lower lip that makes me scream out. I feel the slap to my cheek that makes my ears ring. He never liked when I screamed. That's when the punishments happened.

I can feel the tears welling in my eyes until one escapes down my cheek. I try to push Paxton away, but he thinks I'm grabbing onto him and pulls me in harder, moaning. His hand has now moved from my cheek to my neck and the feeling of his big hand pressed against my throat is what does it. I flail, pushing and scratching, anything to get the hairless man away from me. I can hear the screams of my seven year old self echoing through my head. I grab at my ears and close my eyes begging for it to stop.

"Charlie, Charlie!! What's wrong? What happened?" Paxton's voice breaks through to me and the screaming stops. I open my eyes and look at his terrified face. We are both breathing heavily and I still have tears falling down my cheeks.

"I'm, I'm... I don't... I'm sorry." I try to get the words out but they don't come.

"Shit. I don't know what came over me. I'm sorry I pushed you. I didn't mean to, I just got carried away and I thought you were into it. I'm sorry, please forgive me." I could see the desire and guilt fighting each other in his eyes.

I take a deep breath and stare at Paxton, taking in all of his features and reminding myself that it was him in this car with me, not the hairless man. "It's okay, it's not you. I have my own issues. I just need some time. I'll see you tomorrow." I grab my backpack and with shaky hands manage to get the car door open. My legs feel like jello, but they hold me up as I step out onto the sidewalk.

"I'm sorry Charlie." I look into the car and see him shaking his head and tapping his fingers on the steering wheel. He looks annoyed and I can't tell if it's with me or himself. Probably a little bit of both. "Let me know if you need anything." He says this before putting the car in drive and speeding away.

Shame consumes me as I imagine what Paxton is thinking

right now. I attacked him mid make-out session, and cried in front of him. He probably thinks I'm completely insane. I guess I kind of am.

I make my way into the house. I feel like shit and all I want to do is curl up on the couch and binge eat snacks. I'm on my way to the cabinet filled with junk food when I remember what I agreed to tonight. A date with Gray.

"Ughhhh." The last thing I want to do is go out on a date. I grab my phone out of my backpack and pull up Gray's name in my contact list. I type out a message.

Me: Hey Gray...it's Charlie.

Gray: Hey sweetheart, don't do what I think you're about to do.

Me: What do you mean?

Gray: I have a feeling the only reason you would message me two hours before our date is to cancel on me.

Me: Am I that predictable? Don't hate me...

Gray: I don't hate you, but tell me why you've decided to ruin my day.

Me: Don't make me feel guilty... It's just been a long day and the thought of going out sounds exhausting.

Gray: Okay, no problem. I can work with that ;) Me: What does that mean?

Me: Gray? Why aren't you answering me?

I pick at my nails as I stare at the phone screen. It's been ten minutes since I texted him and he still hasn't answered me. Screw it, I'm not going to stress out over a stupid text that probably meant nothing. Throwing my phone down on the counter I grab a bag of chips and lay down on the couch. I turn on the TV and start flipping through channels. After five minutes of searching, I settle on Friends since there is always a marathon playing. The sound of Ross and Rachel fighting blasts through the speakers and I stare at the lights on the screen.

***

The sound of a doorbell jolts me awake. I must have fallen asleep. The TV is still on and I figure the doorbell came from the show.

Ding Dong.

Shit. That definitely didn't come from the show. I jump off the couch and run over to the front door. Opening it up, it shouldn't surprise me to see Gray's face staring back at me. He's wearing dark blue jeans that are tucked into old combat boots. His grey t-shirt is tight on his body and makes his blue eyes pop. His scruff looks longer today and his hair is as messy as it was last night.

He stands there and looks at me for a second, taking in my appearance. His eyes lazily make their way down my body until they reach a certain spot and then they stop, before he averts his eyes quickly. Confused at what he was looking at, I look down at myself. To my horror, during my nap, my skirt had ridden up far enough to expose the bright pink underwear I was wearing.

"Oh shit." I swear loudly as I pull my skirt back down. "I'm so sorry."

Gray looks me in the eyes before talking. "How did you manage to outdo the towel from last night? You really need to stop answering the door in these outfits." He jokes with a small smirk. "What happens if I'm not the one at the other side of the door next time?" His words make a chill run through my body. He couldn't be more right. Their faces flash in the darkness every time I blink.

"I'm sorry, I fell asleep on the couch and you woke me with the doorbell. I ran and didn't realize my skirt wasn't in place."

"You don't have to apologize sweetheart. Just never pegged you for a bright pink kind of girl." He winks at me and it makes my heart race. "Anyway, I come bearing ice cream, pizza rolls, and a variety of movies for us to enjoy. Anything from rom-coms to horror movies, I've got it all." He holds up two full grocery bags and smiles at me. The smile reminds me of a little boy and I swear I hear another crack in the walls around my heart.

"Are you some sort of stalker? Maybe a psychic or something? How did you know that's exactly what I wanted to do?" He chuckles at my words.

"No, but if I was I'd never admit it." I roll my eyes at his statement. "Anyway, I have a little sister, and when she has a shit day, I know this always cheers her up. Figured it would work for you too. And if it didn't, maybe my charm and good looks would." His eyebrows rise and fall twice as he grins at me. He had that right. His good looks could brighten anyone's day. I can't help but picture him with his little sister, sitting around eating ice cream, and watching movies.

The thought makes me smile and I secretly hope I can see them together one day.

"Alright, you win. But only because I love ice cream. And pizza rolls. And movies." I open the door wider and let him walk past me into the house. He makes his way over to the kitchen counter and sets the bags down.

'So, what happened today, sweetheart?" His question catches me off guard.

"Um. It's nothing. Just a long day." The events that happened two hours ago flash through my mind, threatening to drag me back down with them. I close my eyes and take a deep breath, willing the images of his vile face out of my head. When I open them back up, Gray is standing in front of me.

"You sure you don't want to talk about it? I've seen that look far too many times on people. Something happened, but I don't want to push you. Just know that I'm here." His words feel like a band aid on the deep wounds of my heart.

"Thank you Gray." I can feel the tears welling up in my eyes again. "I'm okay, really. I just have panic attacks sometimes and something happened today that brought out a really bad one." I try to be honest with him without divulging too much of the truth.

Gray reaches out and wipes the tear that falls from my eye. His eyes are frantically searching my own, the desperation to help me present in their blue hue. I watch them move down to my lips and panic takes over. *No, no. I can't kiss someone else right now. Not after that.*

But, instead of desire in his eyes, there is something else. Concern, curiosity, and maybe a little anger?

"What happened to your lip Charlie?" His words are low as he looks at me. I reach up and touch my lower lip, wincing at the pain. He must have bit me harder than I thought. There is a small gash covering my now very swollen lip. I try to suck my lip into my mouth to hide the evidence of what happened. Just one more mark on my body reminding me how screwed up I am.

"Charlie." He is still waiting for an answer.

"It's nothing Gray. I just uh. I um. I got stressed with class-work. I started um. Biting my lip. Yeah. I do that sometimes. It's a nervous tick." I feel horrible lying to him.

He looks down at the cut and stares at it like it will eventually whisper the truth to him. "Sweetheart, there's a very big difference between a small cut from picking your lips and a gash that's put there by someone else." He looks worried, and possibly murderous.

I huff in defeat. "Fine. It's from someone else okay? The panic attack happened when he did it. I was fine and then boom, every-thing came rushing back and I started to freak out. I started scratching and hitting him and I couldn't see him anymore. I only saw them. I just didn't know what to do. I just want to be normal." The words come pouring out, along with the tears. I don't mean to say any of them. Big warm arms engulfed me and instead of feeling panic, I feel comfort. He smells like engine grease and cologne. I cry for what feels like an hour in his arms, until finally the tears stop coming. He pulls away slightly and looks down at me.

"Charlie, a guy did this to you? Did he hit you?" Ugh... He was going to make me say it.

"Um. No... he kind of. He uh... bit me?" Realization splays across his features, and then fury. Fear creeps up my spine at the anger in his eyes and the fact that we are still within inches of each other. Gray must see the fear because his eyes soften and he tries to hide his anger.

"Someone bit you hard enough to leave that mark? Are you, um. Are you into that?" He seems uncomfortable asking the question.

I shake my head as fast as it can move. "No! No way. I don't really know what I'm into, I just know it's not that." I stop and think for a second. "Um... you're not mad? You know that means someone kissed me, right?" The sound of his low laugh makes me look up at him.

"Sweetheart, I'm not mad at you. You just met me yesterday, I don't own you. Do I want to be the one you're kissing? Hell yeah. Does the thought of some other shit kissing you like that make me want to rip his head off? No doubt. But you can make your own decisions and I will respect them." He stops and looks at me for a second. "You said a lot back there Charlie, and I know you probably didn't mean to. I'm not going to pry into your past, because it's clear you have a dark one. But, please don't feel like you need to hide from me. I'm no stranger to living in fear." Hearing those words makes a weight lift off my shoulders.

I reach out and hug him again, thanking him under my breath. He still seems tense, and I can feel the anger radiating off of his body.

"Charlie? What's the guy's name that did that to you?" Gray asks so quietly, I barely hear it. I think about telling him, but I know Paxton didn't mean it. He has been such a good friend and I don't want anything to happen to him.

"It's no one Gray, just some rich kid from school that gave me a ride home. Let's just drop it and enjoy the rest of the night." With a sigh, he drops it and we head over to get the food ready.

Within twenty minutes we are sprawled out on the couch, covered in a blanket, and stuffing our faces with pizza rolls and ice cream while *Horrible Bosses* plays on the TV. We decided to go for a comedy, in light of recent events.

Gray's arm is wrapped around my shoulders and our sides are completely flush against each other. While my body is warm and comfortable, I can't help but notice the tingles that shoot through it whenever he moves against me or his fingers brush against my shoulder. I am trying to pay attention to the movie, but he makes it damn near impossible.

"Tell me about your sister?" I regret saying it the moment it is out in the air. His body noticeably tenses up. He sits up a little straighter and continues rubbing circles on my shoulder with his thumb.

"Her name is Ava. She's thirteen going on thirty." His joke makes me laugh. "She is so smart and she knows it too. She's a pain in my ass." He stops and looks down at me. "Come to think of it, she reminds me a little of you in that sense." I pretend to be offended and punch him lightly on his arm, which only makes him laugh.

"I can tell how much you love her." He smiles at my words and nods his head.

"I would do anything for her. Anything to make sure she was happy and safe." His words seem to hold a deeper meaning, but I don't dig.

"You know we can invite her over here if you want. You said you live right down the block, right?"

Gray looks down at me and kisses the top of my head. "Thanks sweetheart, but no. She doesn't live with me. I live in an apartment a few blocks down on my own."

"Oh I didn't realize. So where do your parents live?" That word coming out of my mouth feels sour, but I get through it.

"Um. My parents died back when I was a kid. Brakes stopped working in their car and they ended up upside down in the woods one night. Our Uncle got custody of us, so she lives with him over on the rich side of town." He has hatred in his voice. I look up at him, feeling guilty for bringing it up. I know how it feels to talk about something so horrible. I didn't realize just how much we had in common.

"Gray... I'm so sorry. I had no idea." I put my hand on his chest, feeling his racing heart, and decide to take a leap. "My parents died when I was seven. The only one left in the family was my Uncle Brian, but he was only twenty one when he got custody of me. I always hated myself for ruining his chances at a normal life." Those words have never left my mouth before.

Gray looks over at me and puts his hand on mine. "You were a little girl, sweetheart. You didn't get a choice in what life handed you, and I'm sure your Uncle was just grateful he still had you." He grabs my hand and kisses it, making butterflies flutter in my stomach. "Thank you for sharing that with me."

We continue the rest of our night in silence, cuddled up on the couch watching comedy movies. At some point, I fall asleep on Gray's chest. Waking up, I feel his steady breathing under my head and peak up to see his eyes closed. He looks so peaceful like this. I continue to stare at his beautiful features, taking advantage of the fact that he can't see me.

"It's not nice to stare, sweetheart." His sleep coated voice makes me jump and turn away. His low laugh fills my ears and then I feel his body move until he is sitting up next to me.

I'm turned away from him, cheeks red from the embarrassment of being caught.

The hair on the back of my neck stands straight up as I feel his breath against my skin.

He grabs the hair falling to the side of my face and tucks it behind my ear before whispering.

"'You can stare at me anytime, baby. As long as I get to stare right back." A shiver runs down my entire body, and my head involuntarily leans into him. His lips just barely graze my earlobe and it makes me gasp. I feel him pull away and I realize my eyes are closed.

"I think I should head out." I can tell he is forcing himself to leave, and I'm thankful he has the strength I clearly don't possess. We both stand up and I lead him to the front door. The oven clock says it's almost eleven pm, which explains why it's pitch black outside. At the door, Gray stops and looks down at me.

"Thank you for letting me crash your night Charlie." He smiles genuinely at me.

"Please, I am the one that needs to say thank you. Seriously… Thank you. For everything. You have no clue how grateful I am that you almost ran me over yesterday." We both laugh.

Gray leans in, turns his head to the side and kisses my cheek. I smile at his sweet gesture, knowing I wasn't ready for anything more right now. "I'll call you tomorrow, sweetheart. Good night."

"Good night Gray." I shut the door as he walks down the front steps. Leaning against it, I take a deep breath. Oh how my life has changed since I moved to Pleasant Grove. The sound of my phone buzzing breaks me from my thoughts. I reach for it and see Gray's name in my inbox. Clicking on the message I can't help but laugh.

Gray: Lock your front door. And change into something else. Like oversized footie pajamas.

His text makes me laugh harder than it should. I decide to be brave and text back.

Me: Door is locked. In the process of undressing now to get those footie pajamas on.

Gray: Don't make me turn this truck around. Get some sleep, sweetheart.

Me: Night Grayson.

CHAPTER 7

Charlie

I wake up the next morning to Uncle Brian singing ACDC's *Thunderstruck* in the shower. The sound makes me laugh. He screams it, making his voice sound raspy. I have to give it to him, he has an impressive voice. Jumping out of bed, I run over to the bathroom door and bang on it.

"Alright Brian Johnson, I have to shower too!" I shout through the door. I hear the water shut off and the curtain open up. The door lock jiggles before it opens and steam billows out of the room. Uncle Brian's smiling face meets mine. He managed to throw on some sweatpants in that short amount of time.

"Holy shit. How did I never realize I have the same first name as the lead singer of ACDC. I should have been a fucking band member!" He starts playing the air guitar in front of me and then bursts out into another song. I am laughing at his little show as he reaches out and ruffles my hair with his wet hand.

"No, stop! You're getting me all wet you jerk." I swat at his arm but instead of pulling away he grabs me in a big bear hug, and successfully manages to get my pjs soaked.

"I just love you so much Char, I can't contain it!" He jokes with me as he shakes his wet hair and the droplets hit my face.

"I'm gonna get you back for this Brian just you wait!" He is walking away from me as I yell at him. He turns around at my words and gives me a wink.

"Please, call me Mr. Johnson, little lady." The air guitar comes back out as he walks backward into his room. I am left laughing alone in the hallway at my insane Uncle. Walking into the bathroom, I take a quick, steaming hot shower, before going back into my room to get dressed. On my way into my room I hear Uncle Brian call up from downstairs.

"Fresh coffee in the pot for you Char. I'm gonna hit the sack. Love ya dork."

"Oh my gosh, Mr. Johnson made me coffee? The rock God himself? I need to write this in my diary!" I joke down the stairs. "Thanks, sleep well. Love you more, loser."

I go into my room and throw on my wrinkled uniform that I left on the ground last night. *Whoops.* I grab the tie that I purposely didn't untie and slip it on around my neck, tightening it slightly, but keeping it relatively loose. I run a brush through my wet hair, trying to tame its frizzy tendrils. Hearing my phone buzz, I grab it off the nightstand.

Gray: Good morning Charlie. Hope you have a great day :)

I smile at my phone. I've never had a guy text me good morning. It was such a simple gesture, but it made me feel special. I quickly type out my response, deciding to joke around with him.

Me: Who's this again?

Gray: Ouch. This is the amazing, smart, sexy man that kept you company last night.

Me: Gonna have to be a bit more specific, there are a lot of sexy men that keep me company at night....

Gray: Are you trying to get me to come whisk you away so I am the only one who can have you? ;)

Me: As tempting as that sounds, I'm just messin with you. No sexy men spending any nights with this girl.

Gray: Excuse me???

Me: Oh. Sorry. There's only one sexy man I spend my nights with. Happy?

Gray: Very. I'll talk to you later, sweetheart Me: Have a great day!

I look back at our chain of messages and smile. I sound like a normal, happy teenager when I talk to him. It's a feeling I've never been able to experience.

I make my way to school and completely forget about the boy who I sucked face with until he is standing right in front of me, blocking me from my locker... again. But this time, Brooke is nowhere in sight. Instead, Paxton stands there alone with his hands in his pockets and a guilty look on his face.

"Charlie..." He looks me in the eyes as he says my name.

"Hey, Paxton. What's up?" I walk past him to my locker, trying to show him that I'm really okay.

"I'm so sorry. I can't stop thinking about what I did. I'm so fucking sorry. I'm the biggest dick in the entire world. I don't know what came over me and I should have-" I cut him off before he can continue.

"Paxton. I already forgave you. It isn't a big deal. I'm not upset about it and I'm not mad at you. So, please, drop it." I lick my lips after I finish talking and his eyes follow the movement.

"Holy shit. Charlotte. I did that?" He comes in closer to get a better look at my lip and I turn my head away from him.

"It looks worse than it is. It doesn't even hurt. Please stop talking about it or I will start completely ignoring you like I did on my first day."

"Okay, okay, fair enough. I'm sorry for the last time ever that I hurt that pretty lip of yours and made you cry. It will never happen again." He smiles down at me and I nod my head with thanks.

We head into class and I zone out the rest of the day. After lunch, I make my way into the girl's bathroom. I hear voices as I sit down to pee, and realize one of them is Brooke.

"He called me yesterday after school. He sounded upset and asked if he could pick me up. It was so random but who's going to say no to his gorgeous face?" She laughs with her friend. "Anyway, he brought me over to his place. Have you ever seen it? Holy shit Christie. It's massive. But, he took me to the little guest house out back and he pushed me up against the wall and just started making out with me. It was so hot... He was so angry and took all that aggression out on me." She stops talking and the other girl whines loudly.

"Ughhh. I'm so jealous. So did you guys go all the way?" Her voice is full of excited anticipation and a hint of annoyance.

Brooke's squeaky giggle fills the bathroom. "Yeah, we did." She sounds so happy as she says it. I sit there and wonder what she must be feeling right now. How it would feel to have sex with someone. To be that passionate about someone. I can tell she likes this person, and I find myself slightly jealous that she is able to put her feelings to action so simply. She didn't have any second thoughts, any demons, any flashbacks haunting her mind as she kissed this man. She just enjoyed it and got lost in the moment. I take the slightly back. I find myself extremely jealous.

***

The rest of the week is filled with the same boring routine and suddenly It's Sunday... my birthday. I have to admit, I don't love the day. Uncle Brian makes them special, and I always have a great time, but it's just a reminder that the people who brought me into this world are no longer in it.

I walk down the stairs, still in my pjs, and find my uncle standing at the dining room table with a huge smile on his face. Behind him is a banner that says happy birthday and on the table is a single chocolate cupcake. It's covered in white frosting and has a lit candle in the middle of it.

"Happy eighteenth birthday Charlotte Briar!!" he screams so loud that I have to cover my ears. I can't help but laugh at his enthusiasm. He grabs the cupcake off the table and brings it over to me. "Make a wish."

I look down at the cupcake and wish for the only thing that I have ever wished for. A wish that will never come true. To see my mom and dad again. I feel tears pricking my eyes as I blow out the candle. I look up to thank Uncle Brian, but before I can get the words out, the perfectly frosted cupcake is smashed right into my face. It takes me by surprise and I don't react for a second. We are both silent as I stand there with cupcake covering my entire face.

"You son of a bitch!!" I wipe some of the cupcake off and chase Brian around the kitchen table as he screams. I catch up to him and slam my hand down on top of his head, rubbing it into his freshly showered hair. He stops in his tracks and turns around to look at me. I wait for him to talk, holding back the laugh in my throat.

"IT'S ON!" he yells before running to the fridge. Oh shit. He pulls out an entire container of cupcakes matching the last one. I panic, searching the counters for something, but come up short. Running to the cabinet, I grab the first thing I see. Reaching my hand into the bag I throw the flour right when he throws his first cupcake at me. The cupcake hits me in the shoulder, frosting coating the strands of my long hair.

"You cheater!" Uncle Brian says as the flour hits him and goes everywhere. He is covered by just the first throw. I watch as he runs toward me and suddenly the entire tray is flying at me and 10 cupcakes hit my front. Brian follows right behind them as he rubs them into my pjs, hair and face. I have chocolate cake and vanilla frosting shoved up my nose, in my ears, and I think it somehow managed to go down my shirt. I am laughing hysterically, with tears streaming down my face.

I stick my tongue out and lick the cupcake off the side of

my face. "Mmmm these cupcakes are delicious," I say through the mouthful of chocolate. Brian looks down at me and laughs, shaking his head.

"Happy birthday, kid. I love you more than anything." He reaches down to help me up and pulls me into a hug. "So, your gift isn't much, but I hope you like it."

"You didn't need to get me anything, you know that." I look at him with a raised eyebrow. I always tell him not to get me anything, and he always ignores it and gets me something. He walks me over to the book shelf and points to the top shelf.

The shelf is filled with all of my favorite books, but a new one stands out from the rest. I pick up the worn book and look at the title: *Pride and Prejudice*.

"It's a first edition. Took me a hell of a long time to find it. But, I figured it would be something you appreciated." He smiles at me, a bit uncomfortable.

"It's perfect, Brian. Thank you so much. This is the best gift you could have given me." I reach out and give him another hug, holding onto the big man as I thank God for allowing me to still have him in my life.

"So, what's your plan for the day?" Brian releases me.

"Well, I figured I'd hangout with you if you wanted... and then, I was going to see if we could invite my friend Gray over?" I say the last part quietly.

"What was that last part?" He raises both eyebrows at me.

"Don't be all weird... His name is Grayson and he's a really good person. You would get along well with him." I am desperately trying to convince him of this fact.

"Oh, I'm sure we will get along just fine. After I threaten his life and manhood." He puts his hand up in the air and starts yelling like a Viking. I roll my eyes, knowing he's joking.

"Ha ha. But, seriously, can he come?"

"Yes, I would love to meet Miss. Briar's new friend Grayson." He puts air quotes around the word friend and I roll my eyes. "Shall we take out our finest china for this momentous occasion? Perhaps I'll have the chef prepare his most exquisite meal. Are three courses enough? Oh, God, what am I saying! Of course it's not. Anything less than five courses just won't do, will it Miss. Charlotte?" He is speaking with the most annoying English accent I have ever heard.

"You're an idiot," I say through my laughter. "But yes, let's do a five course meal of the best take-out Chinese food around. We can order one of everything off the menu, like real classy people do." I stick my pinky in the air and curtsey.

"God... It's a shame you turned out so much like me. You're a freak." Brian tickles my side and we both laugh. "Chinese food sounds perfect. I'll order all of your favorites and then some. We will feast like kings!" I smile at him, loving these moments.

"So, are we thinking movies and junk food all day, or like... go out in civilization and see people... in public... where there are like... people." I try to hold back my laughter as I say the sentence. I want to make Brian laugh, but I'm also not really kidding. I don't particularly want to go out and see anyone today.

"Well, when you put it that way, how could I not want to go out in public?" He shakes his head at me. "What are we feeling? Scary, sad, sappy romance, comedy?"

"I'm thinking, sappy romance or scary."

"Why not do both? We've got until dinner time don't we? Let's get this movie marathon going, birthday girl." Uncle Brian claps his hands and runs to the kitchen. He rummages through the cabinets until he comes back with Oreos, Reese's cups, chips and salsa, and Cheetos. He sets everything on the living room table and then looks back at where I am still standing.

"Oh God, you need a shower first." He plugs his nose and moves his hand back and forth by his face. I flip him off, running up the stairs and hopping into the shower.

We spent the next 5 hours watching *The Conjuring* and then *5 Feet Apart* on Netflix. During the romance movie about two sick people who fall in love, I found myself crying… embarrassingly hard. Brian looked over at me and proceeded to call me a wimp. But, I saw the tears welling up in his eyes and heard the sniffle of his nose at the end of the movie.

Now, we are waiting for Gray to show up with the Chinese. He graciously volunteered to pick it up for us after we ordered it. Uncle Brian turns on the stereo in the living room, and I burst out laughing when the music he chooses blasts through the speakers. ABBA. He chose freaking ABBA. I watch as he snaps his fingers and sways his hips to the music, belting out the words to *Mamma Mia* louder than the girls themselves. I can't help but dance along with him, loving the free feeling I have as my body bounces to the music. We are laughing, dancing, and screaming the words to the music together, when out of the corner of my eye I spot a person standing in the kitchen watching us. I stop dancing and look over.

Gray is standing there, hands full of takeout bags, with the biggest smile on his face. The song comes to an end at that moment and I burst out laughing, bending forward and letting myself roll onto the ground in a humiliated, exhausted ball. I sprawl out on the carpet, and look back over at Gray.

"Hi." Is all I say.

"I'm a bit jealous I missed out on this. I knocked but I think the music was too loud to hear." He puts the bags down and walks over to Brian. "Hi, sir, I'm Grayson. Thank you for letting me join you for dinner tonight."

Brian hesitates to grab the hand that Gray has extended. He looks at him with a glare, and then his expression morphs into a smile and he grabs Gray's hand and shakes it with way too much enthusiasm. "Call me Brian. Glad to meet the person Char is constantly talking so much about." He looks down at me and winks as he says it and my cheeks heat from embarrassment. I flip over onto my stomach so my face is in the carpet and out of view.

"Is that so?" I can hear Gray's huge grin without even looking.

"Stop smiling!" My voice is muffled from the carpet.

I hear them both laugh at me before Uncle Brian says, "Let's eat!"

We shove our faces with Chinese food from chicken lo mein to steamed dumplings, and in between bites we talk. Well, mostly Gray and Brian talk about things like football and the news and oh, yeah, me... like I'm not sitting right next to them.

"She went through a stage where she cut her own bangs and they were always about two inches too short. God, I couldn't stand looking at her for those six months." Brian loves telling all my embarrassing stories, and Gray seems to love hearing them even more.

"Do you have pictures? I would love to see pictures." Gray is smiling from ear to ear.

"They're up in the attic somewhere, I'll have to pull them out one of these days and show you." Brian gets up and walks over to the cabinet above the fridge. He grabs a bottle of Jack Daniels and then reaches for a glass. "Want to join me Grayson?"

"I'd love to, thank you Brian." Gray looks at me and winks, before mouthing to me 'I love your uncle.' I just roll my eyes at him.

"You know what you little dork, I'm gonna pour a glass for you too. You're officially an adult now, so fuck it!" He comes back with three glasses filled with a few ice cubes. He tips the bottle into each glass until they are half full with the amber liquid.

"You ever have whiskey before, Charlie?" Gray asks me as he grabs his drink. I'm about to answer, saying no, when my uncle beats me to it.

"This kid is the biggest damn prude. She always refused to

have a sip of my beer let alone the strong stuff."

"Wow... Thanks Brian." I squint my eyes at him and spit my tongue out. I hear Gray's deep chuckle across the table and can't control the shiver that runs down my spine. I reach for the glass of Jack, trying to distract myself, and take a small sniff. The liquid burns my nostrils and I can't imagine how it will feel going down.

"Alright you little love birds, cheers to Charlotte finally growing up." I cringe at Brian's comment before we all clink our glasses. They both take a swig of their drinks and they don't cringe at all. It looks like they took a sip of water, not straight liquor. Feeling a bit confident from their reactions, I decide it can't be that bad and take a big mouthful.

My mouth instantly wants to spit it out, but I hold it in, forcing myself to swallow. The burn travels all the way down my throat and I cough, as my eyes start to water. The burning feeling continues to travel down into my stomach.

"That bad, huh?" Gray is smirking at me from across the table. I finally contain myself, and after the initial burn, I decide I don't mind it. The taste is pretty good once you get past the feeling of fire in your throat.

"I know it's surprising after my reaction, but I actually kind of like it."

"That's my girl." This statement comes from both Gray and Brian, at the exact same time. They look from me to each other and we all burst out into laughter. I take another sip of my whiskey, and this time it goes down a lot easier and I get to enjoy the slight burn and malty flavor.

It's been a few minutes since we started drinking our whiskey and my head is a bit foggy.

I am laughing at things that I know aren't that funny, and I am talking louder than I should be. I hear Uncle Brian's phone ringing and watch as he stands up and walks into the other room to answer it.

"I didn't think it was possible you could get any more beautiful, sweetheart." Gray's words make my chest warm up even more than it already is.

"Ew, I'm gross right now. I am in my sweats and I just downed half a menu's worth of Chinese food."

"You would look amazing in a trash bag, Charlie." He takes another sip of his drink. "But, I'm talking about the glossy look in your eyes from the Jack. It makes your blue eyes shine even more than they normally do. And the way the tip of your nose is bright pink right now." I reach up and touch my nose. "And just how relaxed and carefree you are. I could stare at you for hours and never get bored."

I'm about to answer him, when Uncle Brian walks back in. "Well, kids. Bad news. Josie cut herself pretty badly on glass at the bar and now I have to go cover her shift." He rolls his eyes as he puts his flannel on. "You guys can hang out here, but no sleeping over... got it?" He points a finger at both of us.

"Of course not, thank you Brian." Gray stands up and walks over to shake his hand. "It was really great meeting you, thank you for tonight."

"The pleasure is all mine." Uncle Brian leans in a bit and tries to whisper, but he's always been a bad whisperer. "You better take care of my girl. She has needed someone besides me in her life for a long time, I'm hopeful that someone is you." He then looks over at me and opens his arms for a hug. I run up to him and hug him as tight as I can.

"Thank you for everything Uncle Brian. I love you so much."

"I love you more Char. I'm so damn proud of the woman you have become." His words make me want to cry, but I don't let myself. I pull away and watch as Brian closes the front door behind him and suddenly we are alone. I'm not sure if it's the whiskey, or just his damn hotness, but all I want to do is push him up against the wall and make out with him, like Brooke described in the bathroom that day. I want to feel his hands all over my body and run my hands along every hard ridge of his. I start to walk toward him, looking his body up and down, when Gray quickly walks toward the table, and away from me. He grabs his whiskey and downs it, before looking back at me.

"I have a gift for you, sweetheart." I smile at his words as he pulls me over to the couch. He reaches into his back pocket and hands me a small black cardboard box. I open it carefully and find a folded up note on top. Unfolding the tiny piece of paper, a few simple words are revealed.

I'm so happy I almost ran you over, sweetheart. -Gray

I smile at the note before I put it to the side. That's when I see a bracelet lying in the box and my heart squeezes. It's made of dark brown leather, almost black, and there is a small carving of a simple rose, surrounded by thorns. Under it are my initials.

"It's a briar rose. Mostly because of your last name, but also because you remind me so much of that rose. You are so beautiful, sweet, unique." He rubs his thumb over my hand. "Soft. Just like that rose. But you're hard to get to because of the many thorns you've put up around yourself. Anyone who can get past those thorns is a lucky son of a bitch, because inside is this magnificent beauty like nothing else in this world." He stops talking and keeps his eyes low. "I'm sorry. That sounded a lot better in my head. Out loud it sounds like a horrible Hallmark card."

"No. No stop. It was perfect." I sniffle, trying not to let tears fall from his sweet words. "This is the most beautiful gift I have ever been given. Thank you Gray." I reach over and give him a hug. He returns it but pulls away before I can try to take it farther. I internally groan as I remind myself that he is just being respectful of my feelings.

***

A loud rumble in the sky wakes me of my peaceful sleep. I jump in my bed, pulling the covers up higher on my body. Lightning strikes and the dark room lights up for a split second. I reach for my phone to check the time. It's 11:30, meaning Gray left an hour ago and Brian won't be home for another 4 hours at least.

I feel my heart start to race as the thunder cracks in the sky again. I hate thunderstorms.

I click on Gray's name and type out a message.

Me: Are you awake?

Gray: Yes, everything okay?

Me: Don't make fun of me… I'm scared of thunder.

Gray: Why are you so cute? Would you feel better if I came back?

Me: YES. I'll unlock the door.

I jump out of bed and race down the stairs as fast as I can. I switch the lock on the front door and spin around, sprinting back up the stairs before the thunder crackles again. I make it back to my bed just in time for the next rumble and this one is loud and shakes the whole house. My heart is racing in my chest and I can feel the beginning of a flashback starting to take over. My vision starts going blurry and my peripheral vision starts to tunnel. *No no no. Not again.*

Right when I start feeling myself going under, a hand grabs my arm and I'm pulled back out. Gray stands in front of me. He is looking down at me, worried.

"You're okay, sweetheart. I'm right here." I sigh in relief and move over in my bed to make room for him. Gray slips his shoes off and gracefully slips into bed with me.

"Take a deep breath, it will be over before you know it. I'll be here with you until you fall asleep." He turns sideways and grabs me, pulling me to him. One of his arms drapes over my chest and he rubs circles on my arm with his fingers. The movement is almost hypnotizing and the thunder starts to sound distant. I hear Gray's steady breathing and my eyes start to close.

His big frame holding me, protecting me, makes me smile and my eyes suddenly feel heavy. I try to keep them open, but sleep wins in the end. Right as I'm drifting to sleep, I feel Gray's lips kiss my temple softly.

CHAPTER 8

Charlie

It's Friday, five days after my birthday. The week was slow and boring. I talked to Gray every day, did school work, joked around with Paxton, and slept... a lot.

Looking down at my new bracelet as I wait for English class to start, I smile to myself thinking about how much my life has changed in the last two weeks. My friendship with Paxton, whatever this thing with Gray is, my new school. It's a little overwhelming, but I can feel myself slowly becoming a normal eighteen year old. I'm lost in thought and don't notice Paxton sneaking up on me in my seat until he grabs at my sides, tickling me and making me jump up with a squeal. I turn around and swat at him, willing my heart to slow down to its normal pace.

"You scared the crap out of me!" I scold him, but I can't hide the smile on my face. He stares at me with an abnormally large smile plastered on his own. "What are you so happy about, weirdo?"

"I thought you'd never ask! Do you have plans tonight?" We both sit down in our seats but he pulls his chair closer to mine and stares me right in the face, smile never faltering. I wanted to hang out with Gray tonight, but he told me he had to work late, so I was planning on reading and going to bed early. I know, what a crazy Friday night. Slow down Charlie!

"Nothing set in stone." I try to sound cooler than I am. "Why?"

"Well, now you have a plan set in stone. I'm taking you to a party tonight, okay? I don't wanna hear any excuses! Everyone is going and that means you have to be there too, as my plus one."

"Paxton, I already told you that I can't date-"

"Plus one as a friend, of course. Nothing more, nothing less. I will talk to you all night, introduce you to people if you want, drive you there and back, the whole shebang. Please say yes." He has his hands clasped in front of him, with his lower lip stuck out. The sight of a huge eighteen year old guy sporting puppy eyes and a pouty lip is actually quite hysterical. I think about what he said. I've never been to a party before. I never had any interest and even if I did, I was never invited. But, I feel like a new Charlie recently, and this Charlie would say yes to a party. At least, I think she would. *Screw it. What do I have to lose?*

"Okay, let's do it!" I should have known I'd regret my decision.

***

I'm standing in front of my mirror, freaking out a little. I have no idea what to wear and Paxton will be here in fifteen minutes. I'm embarrassed to say I googled 'party outfits for high school girls' to find some sort of inspiration for the party. I look down at the three different options I have splayed out on my bed and for the first time ever, I wish I had a girlfriend to help me with this. I decide my next best bet is Gray. He will be honest with me. All three outfits include my ripped black skinny jeans and doc martens, but the shirts are all different. I try on the thick white sweater first before I snap a mirror pic and then try on the cropped Rolling Stones t-shirt and save the one I'm most nervous about for last. I try on the sage green satin tank top that hugs my curves and lays loosely around my boobs. I have never worn this shirt in my entire life. Uncle brain bought it as part of a business casual set for a job interview I had two years ago that I never went to. I take a picture of this one too and quickly send all three pictures to Gray before I lose my courage.

Me: Which one do you like the best?

I wait for his response as I pick at my fingers nervously. After five minutes my phone vibrates.

Gray: Holy shit... You look absolutely stunning in that tank top, sweetheart.

I smile at his text and decide to live a little. The tank top it is. I hear Paxton's car pull up and I run downstairs quickly, locking the door behind me before I change my mind. I jump into the car and right when my butt hits the seat my phone goes off again.

Gray: As much as I love the tank top, you look amazing in the Rolling Stones shirt too. Might be the better option for a party, unless you want guys hitting on you all night ;)

My stomach drops. Why didn't the second text come in before? I suddenly feel cold in my small tank top and realize I haven't said a word to Paxton since I jumped into his car. I look up and find him staring right at my chest. Great.

"You look." His eyes find their way to mine. "Hot." I smile at him and awkwardly use my arms to cover myself up a little, suddenly feeling naked.

"Thanks Paxton, but I think I might-" Before I can finish my sentence, he has the car in drive and all hopes of getting out to change vanish, along with my short-lived courage. "Uh, never mind. Can we turn on some music?" Paxton agrees and music blasts from the stereo, drowning out my racing heart. I pull out my phone.

Me: Your second text came in late. I wore the tank top! What do I do?!?

Gray: Sorry, I have bad service. Just take a deep breath. You're going to be alright, sweetheart, I promise. You look stunning and if you need anything call me. Just stay by your friend at the party. Send me the address just in case you need me?

His text makes me relax slightly. I can do this. I'm eighteen, not eight. Paxton will be right by my side the entire time and I have Gray a phone call away. I ask Paxton for the address and then send it over to Gray before finally putting my phone away. I can do this.

***

I can't do this. We walked into a colonial style house filled with people. I know I go to school with all of them, but I don't recognize a single one. Paxton holds my hand as he leads me through the packed house. My hand is so sweaty I have no idea how he is able to grip it. The music is blaring in my ears, vibrating in my chest, and making my teeth chatter. I have never heard such loud music in my life. We make it to a huge open kitchen and find the counter covered in more alcohol than I have ever seen. Paxton lets go of my hand and starts making a drink while I look around at the people around me.

Everyone is dancing or talking. *How are they talking over this music?* Their dance moves consist of lots of grinding and moving their hips in ways I can't even comprehend. The girls are all dressed in barely any clothes. I swear some of them are wearing lingerie. The guys are all groping or flirting with said practically naked girls. I showed up here worried I was showing too much of my body, and yet I'm the most dressed here. *Ironic.*

"Here you go." I barely hear Paxton yell over the music as he passes a red solo cup my way. I am hesitant to grab it, unaware that he was making me a drink.

"Um... what is it?" I question him as I sniff the contents.

"It's just punch, Brooke made a huge bowl of it," he screams back and I just barely hear the name.

"Brooke?" I question, dreading the answer I know is about to come.

"Yeah, this is Brooke's party!" I didn't have to hear him to know what he said. I put a target on my back with her already and now I show up to her party with Paxton. Just my luck. I lift the punch to my lips and take a few chugs. The sweet, fruity flavor engulfs my mouth and I am so thankful that there are non-alcoholic drinks here. I finish off my drink and feel Paxton's eyes on me. He is staring at me with wide eyes.

"What? I was thirsty," I answer awkwardly. My face feels hot and I can't tell if it's from nerves or the body heat radiating off the hundreds of people surrounding me. Paxton just smiles at me and puts his hands up in defense.

"Want another?" he asks as he reaches for my drink. Tired of yelling, I simply nod my head yes.

I'm halfway done with my second cup of punch when we make our way into another room. It looks like it's supposed to be a living room, but right now it's more of a dance floor.

There are bright flashing lights roaming through the room and it makes my head spin. The farther onto the dance floor we get the more my eyes start to feel heavy and my body lighter. I feel less tense and stressed. The music overwhelms my ears and my hips start to sway to the music at their own accord. I look for Paxton, but he is no longer in front of me, not that I care. I feel too good to care.

Taking another chug of my drink, I start to let my body move however it wants to the music. I let my head fall back and enjoy the numbness. I vaguely feel hands softly grab my waist from behind and assume they are Paxton's. He's my friend, and friends can dance together right? Right now I feel like friends definitely can. He holds my waist a bit tighter as I sway to the Shakira song blasting throughout the room. His hands slowly move lower and I feel my body being pulled back slightly. The room is blurry and my thoughts are scattered as Paxton's body forms to my back. I feel him start to grind himself against me and his attraction is hard to miss.

This doesn't feel right. I shouldn't be doing this, why am I doing this?

I start to pull away but his hands get tighter around me and he holds my hips hard, still grinding into my back. I feel him grab at my hair and pull my head to the side, exposing my neck before a hot tongue hits my skin and bile rises in my throat.

"Paxton! Stop!" I am yelling over the music, but my voice sounds distant to me. I continue to pull away but he is stronger than me. I hear a deep whisper in my ear next.

"I'll give you another guess, hot stuff." The oddly familiar voice hits my ears. I whip my head back to try and see who is still grinding into me and come face to face with John, the guy that made fun of me last week at school. Paxton's friend. "I was surprised when Brooke pointed you out and told me you wanted to dance with me. I thought you were into Paxton." His words barely register. The room is spinning and everything moves in slow motion. Why do I feel like this?

"No... I don't... I don't know what's happening." I can't get my thoughts out.

"Let's go somewhere more private, yeah?" His grip on me tightens even more and he pushes me forward with him. I stumble and trip on my own feet. If he wasn't holding me up I would have fallen. He leads me to a closed door and opens it up, revealing a bedroom.

"Stop, I don't want to. Please." My words are drowned out by the music. I am shoved into the room and I fall to the ground on my knees. My phone flies out of my pocket from the impact and I clumsily grab for it. Searching for his name I can barely make out the letters on my phone as I attempt to text Gray. I press send just as I feel John come up behind me.

"On your knees already? I like the way you think. What's your name again? Shannon?" I hear him more clearly now that the bedroom door is closed.

"My name is-"

"Charlie? Charlie, where are you?" The scream interrupts my sentence as the bedroom door slams open and someone bursts in. "You son of a bitch." I recognize Paxton's voice and turn just in time to see him throw himself on John. The sound of fists hitting skin hits my ears and I take that opportunity to run. I barely manage to stand, but once I'm up I stumble out the door, through the crowd of grabby teens, and out the front door into the cool fresh air.

I sit down on the soft grass and finally take a deep breath. A shiver takes over my body and that's when I notice my chest feels cold and wet. I look down and see red liquid dripping from my satin shirt. The material clings to me and leaves my skin feeling sticky. I didn't realize I spilled my drink on myself. A loud engine and squealing tires pull my eyes away from my shirt and toward the road.

A black Silverado stops right in front of me. I watch as Gray jumps out of the truck and runs over to me. He reaches for my face and cups my cheeks with both hands, looking back and forth between my eyes. He looks crazy. The thought makes me laugh and I hiccup mid laugh. Gray's eyes soften slightly and he rubs his thumb over my cheek.

"You're drunk, sweetheart." His words take a minute to register.

"Noooo. I didn't drink anything. Just fruit punch." I point down at my shirt and giggle. "See? I really want more."

Gray's low chuckle consumes me and I stare up at him. Wow, he's beautiful. Gray starts laughing louder. Shit did I say that out loud?

"Yes, you did. You are beautiful too. And most definitely drunk. That fruit punch you were drinking probably had a shit ton of alcohol in it baby. Let's get you in the truck, okay?" He reaches under my arm and pulls me up, holding most of my weight. Once I'm deposited in the passenger seat the events from tonight come back to me.

"Stupid John. Stupid Brooke. I hate you both." I stick my tongue out the window and flip the house off. Gray watches me with humor on his face.

"What happened, Charlie?"

"Well, Brooke hates me cause I am friends with Axyyyy. I think that's what she calls him? But John was hurting my side. I just wanted to dance. Brooke made John want to dance. Then John didn't want to dance anymore. And I fell in the bedroom. Then, boom, fight." I'm so amazed with how clear and to the point I'm telling the story right now. One point for Charlie, zero for alcohol.

"You're not making any sense baby. Did John hurt you? Tell me who hurt you." Gray's voice is soft but there is an angry edge to it.

"No one hurt me. Really! I'm splenda now that you're here!" I put both thumbs up and smile at Gray. He shakes his head at me and chuckles softly.

"Okay little miss splenda. Let's get you home, shall we?"

I fell asleep at some point on the way home. I vaguely remember Gray lifting me out of the car and putting me in my bed, but besides that, everything is black.

***

I wake up with a pounding headache. The night is a blur of memories that I can't piece together. I look down at my phone and open it up. Holy shit. Ten missed calls and fifteen messages from Paxton. I scroll through the messages.

Where are u?

I'm so sorry, Brooke cornered me and I lost u.

Are u okay?

Charlie, where are u? Am worried sickk! Please answer ur phone.

Coming to ur house.

Ur Uncle answered the door. Didn't know u were at party...but u were in bed already. I'm sorry if I ratted u out... Sorry for tonight.

Oh shit... I'm in for it now. Huffing, I push myself to get out of bed and change out of my sticky clothes. I brush my knotty hair and my teeth and make my way down the stairs, slowly. Of course, Uncle Brian is sitting at the kitchen table, waiting patiently for me. He slides a mug of coffee across the table along with a piece of toast. I sit down and refuse to make eye contact with him.

"Morning sunshine. How are you feeling this beautiful Saturday morning?" His voice echoes through the house as he practically yells the words. The sound makes me wince and I cover my ears. "Oops, is that too loud? Silly me, I should be more considerate of you."

"Okay, okay I'm sorry. I shouldn't have gone to a party, trust me, I regret it completely right now." I reach for the coffee and take a small sip.

"Charlotte. You're eighteen years old. It's completely normal and expected for you to go to parties. But sneaking around? Hiding things from me? That's not acceptable. I'm not the enemy here and I trust you, but you need to trust me and be open with me when you do things like this. You could have gotten really hurt. I had no idea until some guy showed up at the door at three in the morning, right after I got home from work. How did you get home anyway?"

"Gray picked me up and brought me home," I whisper the words.

"I knew I liked that boy. You're lucky he was there for you. And next time, please be honest with me so I don't have to find out from some punk at three in the morning."

"He's not a punk..." I reply a bit defeated.

"He showed up, banging on the door at three in the morning, completely shit faced. I offered to let him stay here and he refused. Some blonde girl was with him and she drove him home thank goodness. That sounds a bit like a punk to me."

I have a feeling that blonde girl was Brooke, but I don't care enough to find out. I sigh deeply and relax in my chair.

"I won't be doing that again anytime soon. But, that punk is a friend of mine and he had the right intentions. I'm sorry I wasn't honest with you. I promise from this point on I will be." Uncle Brian nods his head in understanding before he stands up and places a kiss on the top of my head.

"Eat and drink some water. It will help with the hang-over." With that, he walks upstairs and leaves me alone in my thoughts. Screw being a teenager, this shit is overrated.

CHAPTER 9

Charlie

The next few weeks pass by in a blur. School work has been taking up most of my time. With the end of the school year nearing, everyone is worried about finals and their plans for college. Me? I have no idea what I'm going to do or where I'm going to go. My grades aren't bad, but they definitely aren't scholarship level. And judging by the house we live in, I don't think Brian will be able to help me pay for college, not that I would expect that from him.

My life has been so much calmer with Gray in it. He calls me every night and we just talk about nothing and everything. He asks about the party sometimes, but I refuse to go into it, mostly because I don't 100% remember it. Our dark pasts are also not up for discussion yet, but I am starting to feel like one day I may be able to tell him. My nightmares barely come anymore, and when they do, they are short and manageable. I feel so much lighter. Like maybe, just maybe, I can have a normal life one day.

Paxton has been driving me home from school most days. He watches me like a hawk now and tiptoes around me like I'm going to run if he isn't careful. I haven't brought up Brooke or John, since my middle name is avoidance. Paxton's been doing some avoiding as well. I haven't seen him talk to either of them since that night. He focuses all of his attention on me, and it's obvious he still has feelings for me. But, after everything that has happened, I just can't cross that line with him. Meanwhile with Gray, I am trying to make it obvious that I want the line crossed... Like, now.

He hasn't so much as hugged me in the last few weeks. I know we haven't been able to see each other a lot, with my being busy with school and him busy with work, but I'm starting to worry he only sees me as a friend now. Yes, he calls me sweetheart and beautiful, but friends can call you those things, can't they? Ugh. Why are guys so confusing?

Walking into Chemistry, with Paxton behind me, I take my seat all the way in the back. I see Brooke sitting in her usual seat close to the front, her posture perfect. She throws me a venomous glare and then winks at Paxton. He sits next to me, not acknowledging her and smiles reassuringly at me before taking out his books. Professor Barnes starts talking and I try not to zone out. His voice is so monotone, it's hard not to.

"It's that time, class! Time to focus on our senior projects!" The class collectively murmurs their annoyance. "We will be splitting off into pairs and each pair will come up with their own topic to present. I am giving you free reign on what that topic is, as long as it has to do with one of the chapters in the textbook. Don't make me regret that. You can choose your partner, and for the remainder of class you are free to discuss what your plans are. Good luck."

The class erupts into noise as chairs squeak across the floor and students get up to find a partner. I hate having to pick partners, it always makes my stomach knot up, since I'm never picked and end up having to join another group after the teacher makes them.

"Hey, Paxy!" Her voice screeches through the room and I can't help but cringe. Looking up, I see Brooke bouncing toward Paxton. "Let's be partners! I already have the best idea! We should look into the toxic chemicals in some cosmetic companies. I love makeup and it would totally get us an A!" I watch from my seat as Brooke grabs onto Paxton's arm and I don't miss the way Paxton's eye travel down to the cleavage she is throwing at him. I can't blame him; her boobs are kind of hard to miss.

"As much as I'd love to be your partner and learn all about makeup, I already have a partner." Paxton's voice is cold as he pulls away from her grasp.

"What? Who?" Her voice comes out squeakier when she is annoyed.

"Charlie."

"Who the fuck is Charlie? I don't know a Charlie. I know every guy in this school."

"I'm sure you do, Brooke. Charlie is this beautiful lady right here," he says as he reaches down and pats my head with his hand. Like I'm a freaking dog.

If looks could kill, I'd be dead. Brooke's piercing stare makes me sink down into my seat. I hate confrontation.

"The new girl? Okay it was funny for a while but come on Paxy, can you stop trying to make me jealous? If we're partners we get to be alone together all the time." She gets closer and her voice lowers, but she makes sure it's loud enough for me to hear. "I keep thinking about the other day... I picture us in your bed at night when I'm alone." Hearing that makes my cheeks heat up as I look away and pull out my notebook.

"Brooke, shut the fuck up. It's not happening again and I just told you I have a partner already. I'd hurry up and go find someone else before there's no one left." His voice is quiet but harsh. Brooke stomps her foot like a five year old and then looks down at me and glares.

"Watch your back, bitch," she spits out at me before walking away.

"Hey partner, sorry about that." Paxton pulls his seat closer to my own and leans in.

"I don't think I ever agreed to be your partner, Paxy," I say the nickname in a squeaky voice and Paxton cringes.

"Never ever call me that again," he says as a chill visibly goes through his body. "Her voice is like nails on a chalkboard."

"Clearly it doesn't bother you too much... Based on what she just said." I regret saying it, hearing how jealous I sound.

"Guess you heard that, huh? That was a long time ago and it was a huge mistake. Never happening again. Don't worry Charlie girl, I only have eyes for you." He says the last part as he bats his eyes. I flip him off and open my textbook. I don't really care if Paxton wants to hook up with girls. I know I have feelings for him, but I'm pretty sure those feelings fall in the friendship category. I know I like Gray, there's no question there. He's all I think about. But this thing with Paxton is confusing. Maybe it's because I haven't had a real friend in years, especially a guy.

"Let's figure this project out. What do you want to do?" I ask him in order to change the subject.

"No clue. But we can work on it at my house after school for the next few weeks."

"You mean the mayor's house? Oh my gosh. What will I wear?"

"Ha. Ha. Charlie has jokes now. I almost miss when you just glared at me and refused to talk." His shoulder bumps mine and I stick my tongue out at him. "We have a guest house that my dad lets me use. We can go there to work and no one will bother us."

"Alright, sounds good. But I can't today. We can start tomorrow."

"What? Got a hot date or something?" He laughs at his joke. I decide there's no reason I shouldn't tell him the truth. We are friends after all.

"Uh, I mean it's not a date." I tap my pencil on my desk as I look over at Paxton. His jaw is clenched and he has one eyebrow raised.

"You have a date? With who?" His voice changed from playful to annoyed.

"It's not a date, Paxton. Just someone I'm friends with." Okay maybe I'm not ready to tell him the whole truth. "He doesn't go to school with us. He's a few years older."

"So you're into older guys now?"

"Paxton. I told you because you're my friend too and I want to be honest with you. You don't have to be a dick about it."

"Do you make out with all of your friends?" His words feel like a slap across my face. He pushed himself onto me and I ended up having a panic attack. How could he try to pin that on me? *Screw this.* I push my chair back loudly as I stand up. Grabbing my books, I make my way for the door without saying a word. I hear him calling my name, along with the professor yelling at me, but I ignore it all.

***

I decide to skip the rest of the day, running out the front doors before anyone can stop me. Taking a deep breath of the fresh air, a long walk sounds like just what I need to clear my mind. Today is chilly for the middle of spring, and my bare legs are covered in goosebumps from the wind.

My mind is racing and I can't seem to quiet the noise. I hear Brooke's voice saying she was in Paxton's bed and my stomach knots. I hear Paxton's voice angry and full of hatred. I see the way his eyes judge me as he accuses me of kissing other people. I feel Paxton's lips on mine, torn between desire and fear. The thought of going any further with Paxton scares me. I touch my now healed lip and remember the flashbacks that he caused. When I think of Gray, I feel no fear. I feel comfortable and weightless. I feel safe and beautiful. I love the way he makes me feel, but he treats me like a friend after everything that happened the day Paxton kissed me. When he leaves, he gives me a peck on my cheek. When we are together, he rubs my shoulders and plays with my hair. But that's it. I have never wanted someone to kiss me before Gray. I have never wanted to do anything intimate before Gray. He brings out another side of me. He brings out the beautiful girl on the back of my eyelids. He brings out Petunia.

I laugh at my thought, remembering our first weird interaction. Gray has been this light in my life that I have never had before. I've known him for weeks but it feels like years. I don't know what being in love feels like, but some part of my brain tells me this is it. Which is insane because I barely know anything about him. I don't even know his last name! The more I think about him, the more I know I want more from him. I want to know what it feels like to kiss him. I want to meet Ava and his uncle. I want to know every little thing about him and hold onto him for as long as I can. My heart starts to race at the thought. I need to see him. Screw waiting. I pull out my phone and text him.

Me: Where are you right now?

Gray: Just finishing up a job. On my way back to my apartment. What's up?

I purposely don't answer. Gray showed me where his apartment was when we were driving in his truck last week. Turning around, I pick up the pace as I walk toward our part of town. Ten minutes goes by, along with a missed call from Gray, and I'm right down the road from his place. My heart rate picks up again. A rumble from above has me looking at the sky right when it opens up and cold fat droplets fall towards the ground. It goes from clear and sunny to pouring rain in the matter of seconds. I start to run, trying to avoid getting wet, but by the time I get to his front porch, I'm soaked through. My clothes stick to me as I try to catch my breath. Shaking with adrenaline, I pick my hand up and knock on the door. The thirty seconds it takes for him to open the door feels like an eternity. Then he appears.

"Sweetheart, what's going on? Are you o-" I cut him off before he can finish the question.

"Do you like me?" I am practically yelling so he can hear me over the pouring rain.

"Do I like you? What kind of question is that? Of course I like you Charlie."

"Then kiss me." My bravery shocks me as the words leave my mouth. He stares at me for a second, looking back and forth between my eyes, deciphering if I'm serious. The rain continues to pour as he steps out onto the front porch, soaking his clothes within seconds.

Water drips from his curly black hair as he positions himself mere inches from me. My breathing is labored, my eyes refusing to leave his. Warm hands slide up my arms, over my shoulders, past my neck, and land at the sides of my face. His thumbs wipe water from my cheeks, leaving warm tingles in their trail.

"Are you sure, sweetheart?" His voice is low and I barely make it out through the rain. All

I can do is nod my head yes. His eyes move down to my lips, and I watch as he licks his own. His head dips down until we are nose to nose, but our lips don't touch. His warm breath mixes with my own and my whole body feels like it's on fire.

"You're so beautiful." I barely hear the whisper before his lips touch mine and my heart stops beating. My eyes flutter closed and everything around me disappears. I can't hear the rain anymore. I can't hear the cars driving by. I can't feel the cold drops soaking through my clothes. All I feel is him. His warm hands holding my face to his. His soft lips slowly dancing across my own. Tingles shoot up my spine as I reach up and grab his head, threading my fingers through his hair. His lips caress mine gently, as if he is trying to memorize the feel of them. Every curve, every line, every movement they make. Wanting more, I open my lips up just slightly, inviting him in. He pulls back slightly and his heavy breaths drift across my lips.

"We can stop, baby." He barely gets the words out, his eyes looking into mine from the close proximity. I shake my head no, frantically, as I step in even closer to him, pulling his head towards mine. I barely hear his low chuckle through the rain, but I can feel the vibration and it sends heat down to my toes. His hands guide my face to his and the soft gentle kiss is gone. In its place is a passionate kiss that makes my toes curl. I can barely catch a breath as he devours my mouth. His taste is addicting, a cross between coffee and chocolate. Our bodies are flush together as he guides me until I feel something at my back, I'm assuming the front door, and he pushes me up against it. I'm lost in everything Gray. His touch on my neck. The way his hands grab at my hips. Our height difference makes me go up on my tippy toes, trying to get closer to him. Without breaking the kiss, Gray grabs me by the back of my thighs and pulls me up until I'm pressed between him and the door. I am so caught up in his kiss that I forget to worry about my weight in his hands. He makes me forget everything I've ever feared. All the black shadows that consume me are gone, and the only thing left is Gray.

CHAPTER 10

Paxton

I feel like the biggest dick in the world. I let my jealousy get the best of me, and now Charlie's hurting. More than she already was. I have no idea what happened to her or where she came from, but she clearly went through some shit before showing up at Pleasant Grove. Shit that she won't tell me. She is such a breath of fresh air compared to the other girls in this school. I'll admit, I've used some of these annoying brats for sex countless times, like Brooke, but no one has ever made me feel the way Charlie does. When I make her laugh, everything else disappears. The way her lips felt on mine... Fuck me. I think about it almost every night, wishing we could have gone farther, but knowing I pushed her past her limit.

Pulling up to the gate at our house, Toni, the gatekeeper, waves and the gate opens. I have the urge to turn around, regretting that I didn't follow Charlie when she left. I should have gotten up and chased after her, but I didn't want to risk my perfect attendance. I know it's stupid, but I can't risk anything ruining my chances at going to Harvard. My dad will think I'm a failure if I don't go to the best of the best...

Walking into the house, I make my way to the kitchen. Gina, our chef, is already making food when I arrive.

"Hi Mr. Whitlock. I already have some grilled cheese on the stove top for y'all. Miss, Avery requested one and I figured you would want one as well." Her voice has a slight southern twang.

"You're the best Gina, thank you. Where is Avery?"

"I think she is in her room, on the phone with someone." She doesn't stop cooking as she answers me.

She's probably on the phone with her asshole brother. I fucking hate him. We grew up together and we used to be best friends. But, the minute we became teenagers he started treating me like shit. He glared at me, ignored me, and became so distant that I barely ever saw him. He would constantly disrespect my dad and I would defend him, which only made the dick hate me more. Part of me misses the old him, but the rest of me despises him. Avery, on the other hand, well, I considered her my sister. I would kill anyone who tried to hurt her.

Once I finish eating my sandwich, I thank Gina again, and make my way to the guest house. On my way out, I hear my dad's voice coming from his office. He is whisper yelling and I can barely make out the words.

"You better fucking answer your phone shit head." I miss the next sentence. "I'm this close to-" Then jumbled words. "You'll never see her again. I own your pathetic ass." He goes quiet after that last comment and I assume he hangs up. Who the hell was he talking to? I know he has to be tough to get what he wants in the game of politics, but that didn't sound right. Usually he's the master of negotiation, and if that doesn't work he'll occasionally gamble in light political blackmail to get what he wants, but that didn't sound like politics.

I decide to drop it and go get some homework done. I walk into the small studio style guest house. It's all one big open area with a small kitchen, living area, bedroom, and then a bathroom closed off in the corner. I throw my bag down on my bed and head over to the fridge. Opening it up, I scan it for something to drink. Through the many bottles of beer, I finally find one lone bottle of water and grab that. My mind is still thinking about Charlie's hurt eyes as I open up my Calculus textbook and try to get some work done.

Two hours go by and I've barely gotten anything done. I grab my phone and scroll through my contacts until I reach the name *Charlie girl.* I decide to text her.

Me: Charlie, I'm really sorry for what I said. I don't know what it is about you but I always seem to do and say the wrong thing when I'm around you. I hate that I hurt you when we were kissing, that was never my intention. I'm sorry I lost you at the party and John did what he did. And I'm sorry I got super jealous earlier today. I trust you, and I know we are only friends... But I like you a lot and I hope maybe one day we can be more. But either way, I don't want to lose you.

I click send before I change my mind. Re-reading the message I regret it instantly. I sound like such a pussy. A desperate psycho. Great. My phone buzzes five minutes later.

Charlie girl: Apology accepted.

I sit there and contemplate if I should respond. Fuck it.

Me: Thank you, expect a big hug in the am. What are you doing now?

I wait fifteen minutes before checking my phone for a message. But, there's nothing. That's when I realize she is probably hanging out with her older "friend". I roll my eyes, trying not to get jealous. *Let it go Paxton. You'll see her tomorrow.* I throw my phone on the bed and stand up, heading to the fridge. Time to drown my jealousy in beer.

CHAPTER 11

Gray

I look over at her sitting on my couch with her knees folded under her. She is so focused; her eyebrows are furrowed and she's biting her bottom lip. I can still feel her lips on mine, taste that bottom lip she is so intently biting. Her hair is thrown up into a messy bun on top of her head, and she is now in one of my t-shirts and a pair of boxers since her clothes were soaked through. It's by far the sexiest outfit I've seen on her yet, and I am in awe of my restraint. All I want to do is rip her shirt off and continue what we started earlier. But I know she's not ready for that.

"Are you going to go anytime soon?" I tease her. She manages to tear her eyes off the scrabble game in front of us to glare at me.

"There's a reason I'm winning, Grayson. It's because I take my time and don't make any impulse decisions."

"No impulse decisions huh? Miss 'shows up at my door and practically begs me to kiss her'." I grab her hand and hold it in mine. Being with her feels so natural. It almost makes me forget the rest of my life. "Almost" being the keyword. My phone has vibrated three times since Charlie surprised me, and I know exactly who it is. I have a job to do tonight, even though all I want to do is stay here with her. But, I have Ava to think about. She is my top priority, and always will be.

"Screw you, I took a chance and I think it worked out in my favor." Her smile beams at me.

"Say that first part again? But in the form of a question, and instead of the word you, say me. Please?" I put my hands out in front of me in a pleading gesture. She just laughs and shakes her head, looking back down at the scrabble board. Finally she goes and it's my turn. I can hear my heart starting to pound as I add on to the word "girl" on the board. I wait for her to read it out loud.

"Girlfriend? Impressive." She starts counting up the points, but I grab her chin and make her look me in the eyes.

"So will you?" My voice is low.

"Will I what?" Confusion covers her beautiful face.

"Will you be my girlfriend, sweetheart?" I hear her gasp quietly as she blinks at me. She doesn't speak at first, and I worry I asked too soon, or I'm pushing her too far. I'm about to take it back, telling her it's all a joke, when I see her lips turn up into a small smile.

"I've never been someone's girlfriend before." She doesn't answer the question directly. I laugh at her and rub my thumb over her cheek.

"So, is that a yes?"

"Yes, I would love to be your girlfriend Grayson." Her smile looks like the damn sun and I steal a kiss quickly, knowing I have business to get to soon. She pulls me in for a hug, and I hold her there for a few minutes.

"I'm sorry to do this babe but I got a call saying I have to head into work for a bit." I start to stand, pulling her up with me.

"That's okay, I should be getting home anyway." Her smile doesn't fade as we make our way to the front door. "Oh, I have been meaning to ask. I should probably know my boyfriend's last name, right?" She laughs at her joke, but expects an answer.

"Oh is that a requirement? Shit... I take it back then." I pinch her side as she giggles next to me. "My last name is Lock."

"God, even your last name is hot." She pretends to fan herself off. "Oh, by the way, I have to go over to my friend's house for a stupid school project tomorrow, so I won't get to see you." She makes an exaggerated pouty face.

"That sounds like a blast. Can I come?" I make a joke, all the while discreetly trying to get her to hurry up so I can leave, for Ava's sake.

"Oh you're more than welcome. His dad is apparently the mayor, so after tomorrow I'll pretty much be royalty." Her sentence replays in my head as my ears start to ring. *His dad is the mayor.* My Charlie is friends with that piece of shit. My Charlie is going to be in the same house as the devil himself. I feel bile rise in my throat as I realize the girl I love is walking right into the lion's den, and she doesn't even know it.

CHAPTER 12

Charlie

Paxton's Porsche pulls up to a gate and a man waves at us as he opens it up. I'm already intimidated and I haven't even seen the house yet. The car slowly climbs up the windy paved driveway, surrounded by perfectly landscaped lawn, until the house comes into view. Holy shit. A huge red brick neoclassical home looms over us with white columns aligning the front. The windows are all lined with black shutters and the black double front door has to be at least fifteen feet tall. I gulp down my nerves and try to act unaffected by the mansion in front of me.

"Hey, you okay?" It's like my nerves are radiating off of me.

"Yeah, just a little intimidated by the mansion you call your home."

"Yeah, my dad is a bit over the top with everything he does. Don't worry, we will skip the house tour and go straight to the guest house out back if that makes you feel better." I nod my head yes as he parks the car at the end of the horse shoe shaped driveway.

We make our way past the house, down a cobblestone path. There are white roses adorning each side of the path, along with multiple white arches that are covered in vines. The back of the house is just as spectacular, with a huge rectangular pool, matching hot tub, and covered gazebo. There is a table that could sit twenty, and a top-of-the-line grill sits next to a brick pizza oven. The guest house, which appears to be the same size as my house, sits at the end of the cobblestone path. It matches the main house, with the red brick, and black shutters covering the windows. We go through the front door and it is filled with gorgeous neutral colored furniture that clearly costs a fortune. Living area is to my right, with a tan plush sectional and a TV that reminds me of the movie theater screens. The dining room is to my left, with a six person wood table, which flows straight into the open kitchen. There is a king size bed positioned to the right of the kitchen, with the bed facing the large TV in the living area. The bedspread is the same color as the couch, and there are about twenty throw pillows perfectly placed on top. It looks like the comfiest bed I have ever seen. There is a single door in the back, which I presume is a bathroom.

"Wow Paxton. This is where you get to live?" I can't stop looking around the perfect home.

"Yup. This is home." He makes his way to the kitchen, opening up the fridge. "Want something to drink? I have beer, water, and beer." I watch as he grabs a beer out of the fridge for himself. I've never had a beer, and I don't think today is the day to start. We need to focus.

"I'll have a water please." I walk over to him and reach for the water in his hand as I thank him.

"Alright, let's get this shit over with." He leads me over to the couch and we set our textbooks out on the coffee table. Sitting down, we get to work.

Hours go by, along with over half of our project being finished. Turns out, we work really well together. We got off topic a few times, joking around with each other, but we were able to focus enough to get most of our work finished. Leaning back on the couch and huffing loudly, I relax into the soft cushions. I hear a loud knock on the front door and my body tenses as I sit up straight again.

"Come in." Paxton's voice echoes through the house as the door opens. A large man walks in with salt and pepper hair styled perfectly on his head. He is dressed in a tailored navy blue suit, which shows off his impressive build underneath. His mouth is plastered in a smile, but something about it makes me shiver. I bring my eyes up to his own, and goosebumps prickle my skin. His dark beady eyes stare right into mine. At first glance, he looks like a kind, preppy man in his early 60's. But, the darkness in his stare and the way he looks me up and down as I sit here, makes my skin crawl.

"Ah you must be Charlotte. I've been looking forward to finally meeting you." His voice sounds oddly familiar, and I swear I have heard it somewhere. I search in the deepest depths of my memory, but come up short.

"Uh, Yes... Hi, sir. I'm Charlie." My voice comes out quiet. I look up into his eyes as I introduce myself and I swear I see a flash of something I can't quite read in his eyes when I say the word sir. Maybe I just imagined it.

"I just came out to say hello before I leave for my meeting. I wanted to finally meet the famous Charlotte Briar."

"Jeez dad, enough. Bye, thanks for stopping in." Paxton rolls his eyes at his dad's comment. If I wasn't so distracted by this man's sinister stare, I may have laughed at his embarrassment.

"Alright I'll leave." His dad chuckles as he turns and grabs for the door. Right when he is about to step out of the house, he stops and turns his head around to look into my eyes.

"I'll be seeing you soon, Charlotte." And with that he leaves. My heart is racing and my mouth is dry. The worst part is I don't even know why I'm reacting like this to his dad. If he's anything like Paxton, he is probably a great guy. I replay the interaction in my head again and realize everything he said to me was polite. So why do I have this overwhelming feeling of dread?

"Charlie girl? You okay?" Paxton's voice breaks me from my thoughts.

"Yeah, um, I'm okay. I have to head out though. Mind driving me home?" Paxton's eyes move between my own.

"Sure, grab your bag and let's head out."

***

I spend the next few days with Paxton, working on our project. Luckily, I haven't seen

Paxton's dad since the first day. I don't know if I could handle another weird interaction with him. It's now day three and my brain feels like jello. I never want to think about Chemistry again.

"Charlie girl!! We did it! We're done!" Paxton jumps off the couch and dramatically pumps his fist into the air. I laugh and shake my head at him.

"You're such a loser," I joke. He stops his fist pumping and looks down at me on the couch.

"What did you say?" His mouth curves up in a smirk as he slowly stalks toward me. Before I can answer he scoops me up in his arms, throwing me over his shoulder. My scream echoes through the room before his hands start tickling my sides and that scream is replaced by hysterical laughing.

"Stop, please!! I can't breathe!" I get the words out between cackles. He stops tickling me but doesn't let go of me. Instead, he walks me over to his bed and throws me on it. I'm still laughing when my back hits the bed. I watch as Paxton stands there watching me. The humored look in his eye changes and I know I have to speak up. He starts to lean down, putting himself above me on the bed and the desire in his eyes intensifies.

"Paxton, wait." I put my hands up to block him from going any farther. "I need to tell you something."

He stops leaning in and looks down at me. "I have wanted to

kiss you again for so long Charlie girl, please tell me you're ready now." He is staring me in my eyes and there must be something in them that reflects my actual feelings. He moves away and sits down on the bed next to me.

"There's someone else... isn't there?" He doesn't look at me when he speaks.

"I'm sorry Paxton. I should have told you sooner but I didn't know what my feelings were for you. I'm not used to having guy friends and I couldn't decide if I liked you as a friend or something more... I know now that it's as a friend." I take a deep breath. "You're one of the best and only friends I've ever had and I don't want to lose you."

"Who is he, Charlie? You owe me that" His words are cold.

"You probably don't know him... He's older than us. But, his name is Grayson." I see something change in Paxton's face when I say Gray's name. He recognizes the name.

"Are you fucking kidding me?" He stands up and walks toward the fridge, grabbing a beer.

"What? Do you know him?"

"Do I know him?" He laughs as he shakes his head. "I can't fucking believe this shit." He chugs the beer and then goes in for another.

"Paxton, please, talk to me." My stomach is doing flips.

"Good luck with that one. He's a fucking asshole who only cares about himself." His words hit me hard. "I can't do this right now. I'll have a driver take you home. Just get out."

"Paxton... please." I can feel tears in my eyes.

"Go Charlie." There is pain in his eyes and I feel like the biggest ass in the world. I hate that I am hurting him.

I have no idea how he knows Gray, but he clearly knows a version of him that I've never seen. I want to ask again, to figure out what's going on, but I know I can't. I grab my backpack off the couch and walk toward the door. Before I leave I look back and say I'm sorry one more time before walking out.

I'm walking on the cobblestone path leading to the front of the house when I see a truck zooming down the driveway. It's going too fast for me to get a good look, but I swear its Gray's black Silverado.

Why would he be here?

CHAPTER 13

Gray

My tires squeal against the perfectly paved driveway. I am gripping my steering wheel so tight it hurts. The asshole in my passenger seat just stares ahead with a smirk. I know Charlie has been with Paxton every day after school for the past few days, and I can sense she is here now. I hate leaving the two girls I love in his house, but at least I have the devil himself with me instead of there with them.

He called me this afternoon telling me we had to talk. I have no idea what he wants to talk about. I already do all of his dirty work, what else could he want? We pull up to Angelo's, the Italian restaurant he regulars. Sitting at his usual table, he orders a Manhattan and I order straight Jack. He waits to start talking until our drinks are served and we are left alone.

"I met the most beautiful young lady the other day. She's at the house right now actually." Richard's voice breaks the silence. My teeth clench, knowing he is referring to Charlie, but I try to control my temper. I don't need him knowing I have any attachment to her.

"That so?" I take a sip of my Jack, enjoying the burn as it runs down my throat.

"Her name is Charlotte Briar. My son is trying to get in her pants. Honestly, I'd love to get that girl under me too." He stops and snickers to himself and I feel my blood boiling. I'm gripping my drink so hard I swear the glass may crack into a million sharp little shards. "Anyway, I've been searching for the little bitch for a long time now. Ten fucking years to be exact. But, my guys finally found her. Living in some shitty part of Massachusetts with her pathetic drunk of an uncle. I offered him the chance of a lifetime for her with a full ride scholarship to the most prestigious school around, and he brought her right to me." His words aren't registering. How does he know Charlie? What could he possibly need from her?

"Why? What's so special about this girl?" My anger is coming through in my voice, but he's too focused on his drink to notice.

"She belongs to a very powerful man. A powerful man who is paying a lot of money for her, and has been waiting for the last ten years." He talks about her like she's property. I know what he's referring to now. The part of the business I don't touch. The part I told him I would never help him with. His child/sex trafficking business. He only dabbles with it occasionally, so I have been able to avoid it until now. I feel the jack rising back up in my throat. I swallow it back down, trying to control my anger and fear.

"What does this have to do with me?" The words burn as I say them. I hate sounding so unaffected after hearing him say Charlie belongs to one of his sick and twisted clients.

"You're going to gain her trust Grayson, and you are going to bring her to the drop off spot in two weeks. The drop off is in New Hampshire, at my private landing strip on the shoreline. Her owner has been in Russia for the last month, but he will be back in Portugal at the drop off date. The most discreet way to get her to him is by private jet from my landing strip. He has a jet that will be waiting for you. It's your job to get her on it. My men failed the first time, and I won't let that happen again." He takes a sip of his drink, acting like we are talking about a football game and not the sale of another human being.

"I've told you before that I will never be involved in this part of your fucked up business. Need me to deal your drugs? Fine. Need me to beat someone up for you? Whatever. But helping you sell someone like they are property? I drew that line with you from the start." I try to sound as strong as possible, but I can hear the shakiness in my voice.

"True." He sounds so calm. Too calm. "But I figured this time I could convince you."

"How's that?" I spit the words at him.

"If you don't deliver Charlotte to my client, your darling sister Avery will be sold to the highest bidder. Have you talked to her in the past 24 hours, Grayson?" Fear fills my entire body. I had texted Ava this morning but I never heard back.

"What did you do?" I'm no longer controlling my feelings and I'm two seconds away from grabbing him by the throat.

"Oh don't worry, she's having the time of her life. It just so happens the school decided to take a last minute field trip for Ava's Spanish class. Funded by their loving mayor. Where did they go again? Oh, yes, Spain. They left today and will be gone for a few weeks." He starts to laugh maliciously.

"It would be a shame if she got lost on the trip and ended up in the wrong hands." I feel tears pooling up in my eyes, but I don't let them fall. "You are the only one who can bring that girl home. Get Charlotte on that plane, and Ava will be back with the rest of the kids."

I am breathing heavy; my mind is a complete maze of thoughts. I'm trying to think of a way out of this and nothing comes. He owns everyone, has control over everyone, including me. He could easily get Charlotte on that plane himself, but he's trying to ruin me. He wants me to be involved in every sick game he plays. He wants me to know I'm powerless.

"I have men who will be watching you these next two

WHEN A ROSE FALLS

weeks." He nods his head over to two middle aged men in a booth, watching us. One has dirty blonde hair, buzzed short, and the other is completely bald. "I told them not to interfere, but they will be making sure you get the job done."

I down the rest of my drink, heartbeat filling my ears, and throw my chair back, standing up. Without a word I walk away from the man who has ruined my life. I need to think. To come up with a plan. A plan to save my girls.

CHAPTER 14

Charlie

I scroll through my messages with Gray from the last few days. He is giving me a lot of one word answers. I can tell something's wrong but he won't tell me what. It's been four days since I thought I saw his truck at the mayor's house, and I haven't seen him once. I haven't seen Paxton for that matter either. I have texted him a few times, but he hasn't responded. I'm hoping he just needs time and doesn't hate me forever. I have been spending most of my time reading, thinking about both of them, and reading. I can't lose either of them. Paxton is my best friend and I think I'm falling in love with Gray.

I walk down the stairs and see Uncle Brian sitting at the dining room table drinking a cup of coffee.

"Hey stranger, haven't seen you in a while," he jokes. With our schedules, I almost never see him.

"Is there more coffee?" I ask as I bop him on the head walking past him.

"Fresh pot, I can make some breakfast too if you want." He always offers to cook, but he can barely boil water let alone cook an entire meal.

"You're gonna cook, huh?" I glance over at him as I grab a cup

"Yeah, I actually found this really great recipe I have been meaning to try out. It's so simple. You just pour some cereal in a bowl and then cover it with milk. It's foolproof!" He always knows how to make me laugh.

"I have a strange feeling you would manage to screw it up anyway. How about I make some real breakfast? Eggs and bacon sound good?"

"You're the best Char." He smiles at me before looking down at the paper that is now in his hand.

Once we finish eating, Uncle Brian looks at me like he wants to say something. "What's up?" I ask him.

"This guy you're seeing, Gray, you really like him huh?"

"Oh God, let's not do this Uncle Brian." I know where he is going with this.

"I just want you to be careful. I'm so happy you're happy and experiencing life the way you should be, but I want you to be safe." He reaches into his pocket for something and I am horrified by what he drops on the table. A condom.

"Ughhh stop!" I am trying not to laugh as my entire face heats up from embarrassment.

"You were actually being really sweet for a second and then had to ruin it with the condom."

"I know, I know. You're a smart girl but I just want to make sure you don't get yourself into something you can't handle. Just take it, for me." He passes it over and I pretend to gag as I pick it up with two fingers and hold it far away from me. He laughs at my dramatics and shakes his head. Deciding I can't handle anymore gifts from my uncle I jump up and kiss him on the cheek before heading up to get dressed. I am going to go see Gray, whether he likes it or not.

***

Walking down the block, I spot his truck sitting outside his house. I get the same nervous butterflies I always get when I see him, but I also feel anxiety bubbling up. What if he lost interest in me and that's why he's been so distant? What if he realized I'm too young? Too fucked up? Not skinny enough or pretty enough? I run through all of these what ifs until I reach his front door. Knocking, I push down all of my feelings of doubt and wait for him to answer it.

I watch as the door opens and Gray comes into view. Only, he doesn't look like my normal happy Gray. He has bags under his eyes and his hair looks greasy. His clothes don't appear to be as snug as they usually are. Has he been eating? He has worry in his eyes and I can tell he hasn't been sleeping.

"Holy shit, Gray are you alright?" I push past him into the house and grab onto his hand so I can drag him over to his couch. Sitting him down in front of me, I look over his features again.

"Yeah. I'm fine. Just a lot going on Charlie. I… I'm fine." He rubs my cheek with his thumb, but his eyes barely reach mine.

"Gray, please let me in." I feel tears in my eyes at this man's pain. I hate seeing him hurt.

He stares at me for what feels like hours and then he takes a deep breath.

"That day I met you, sweetheart? You were so scared, your eyes looked so empty. I wanted to scoop you up and hold you close to me. Take away all of the pain in your past. Make sure no one ever hurt you again. I've never felt that way about anyone except for Ava." His eyes close at her name. "But, now? You're so much stronger. You have this bright light that comes out every time you smile or laugh and it's contagious. Every time I'm with you I forget all of the shit in this world and the only thing I see is you. You have made me happier than I have ever been in my life Charlie Briar. You're the best thing that's come into this horrible little town." He pauses and looks down at his lap.

"Why are you saying this, Gray?" I tell myself the tears falling down my cheeks are from the kind words he says, but I know it's from the fear of what he's about to say to me. I can't shake the feeling he's about to end this whole thing. He doesn't answer me, looking down at his lap still. I see a single tear fall from his face and land on his gray sweatpants, and I can't help but reach for his hand. He lets me take it and then his eyes meet mine.

"I love you Charlie." The words steal the oxygen from my lungs. That was the last thing I expected him to say to me. He loves me. Someone actually loves me. The feeling is so over-whelming I can't find my voice to answer him. The walls around my heart crumble into a million pieces and my heart feels so full it may explode.

"I love you too Grayson." I barely get the words out as I reach over for his face and pull him in for a kiss. He kisses me back, but grabs my face and pushes me back just enough to talk.

"I want to kiss you so bad, but I also need to take a shower because I smell like trash." I let his words sink in before I let the next sentence leave my mouth.

"Okay, let's go." I look him in the eyes and don't back down, letting him know I'm serious.

"Together? Are you sure baby?" I see the heated look in his eyes, but also the apprehension.

"Yes." I stand up and wait for him to grab my hand. He reaches for it and we walk toward the bathroom. I can feel nerves and excitement swirling around in my stomach as Gray flips the light switch on and the fluorescent lights make my eyes squint. The bathroom isn't huge. To the left of the door there is a double sink with a mirror and a toilet. Straight ahead the glass walk-in shower stands, waiting for us.

I gulp as the realization of what I'm about to do sinks in. No one has ever seen my body in this way. I have dimples in my skin, scars on my body, and I'm not as skinny as I want to be.

He is going to think I'm ugly. He's going to look away the minute he sees what I actually look like under these clothes. He's going to-.

"Stop thinking. Don't go where I know your brain is. You're the most beautiful woman I have ever met, both inside and out. If you aren't ready for this, we won't do it. But if you are worried about the way you look, throw all of those thoughts away. Because you're perfect in my eyes." His words feel like a warm blanket being wrapped around me.

"How'd you know I was thinking about that?" I smile up at him in awe.

"You had that look in your eyes. The 'I'm not good enough' look. I have seen it on your face too many times to count. If I have to convince you for the rest of my life that you are the one that is too good for anyone else, including me, I will."

Instead of answering him, I look him right in the eyes and reach for the buttons on my cardigan. Slowly, I keep eye contact as my fingers shakily attempt to undo each small button. I am fumbling over my own fingers when Gray's warm, big hands cover mine. I let my hands fall to my sides as he undoes the rest of my sweater. He then grips the collar of it and slowly drags the sleeves down my arms. His fingers graze my sensitive skin, making me shiver in my thin tank top. He slowly moves down to the hem of my white tank, and the fabric peels off my skin. I raise my arms above my head so he can easily remove it. Standing in front of him, in my black lace bralette, with my scars on show, I start to feel too exposed and put my arms over my chest, trying to cover up. Gray stares at me, grabbing my arms and putting them back at my sides where he holds them there. His eyes slowly rake over my body. Staring at my chest, and then taking in every horrible line that covers my middle half. There are long jagged scars from the sick bastards carving into me. There are imperfect circles scattered across my abdomen and back from the many cigars they put out on me. I swallow down the memories, refusing to let them ruin this moment.

Gray bends down and kisses my mouth softly. Before I can

intensify the kiss, he pulls his lips away and I whimper. But, his lips don't go far. He places hot kisses across my jawline, over to my ear. He kisses my ear lobe before putting it in his mouth and biting softly. The feeling pulls a moan out of my mouth as I grab onto his arms and close my eyes. His mouth trails down my neck as he sucks softly and kisses his way lower. His hot breath hits my chest, and I feel his hands reach behind me to my bra clasp. He gets it open in one swift motion and the bra falls between us. His eyes stare at my bare chest. I swear I see actual fire in his stare, and it burns into my skin in the most delicious way. He bends his head back down and kisses his way across my breasts, sucking and biting softly, making my knees weak.

His mouth moves lower still, and I start to tense up. He is at eye level with all of those painful memories. Every single mark tells a story... A story I wish I could forget. I look down at him as his eyes graze across my skin, taking in each mark. He looks up at me and stares into my eyes.

"You're the most beautiful thing I've ever laid my eyes on, sweetheart." His words bring tears to my eyes, but I hold them in. He looks back down and starts kissing my scars, taking in every one, gently pressing his lips to their rough, jagged lines. I can't control the tear that escapes and runs down my cheek. He is my everything. I have never felt this kind of love in my life.

He stands back up and goes over to the shower, turning it on. I watch him as he pulls his t-shirt over his head. The intricate black tattoos on his arms fade onto one side of his chest. There is a detailed, faded tattoo of a lion, with his mouth baring its teeth right over his heart. It's the sexiest thing I've ever seen. Actually, scratch that. His tan abs and dark happy trail leading into his gray sweatpants is. My entire body feels like it's on fire as he puts his hands in the waistband of his sweats and he pushes them down, across his muscular legs until they pool at the ground. He steps out of them and I stare at the ground for a few more seconds before trailing my eyes back up. His black boxer briefs are tight on his toned body. The huge bulge that constricts against the black fabric makes my heart race. I've never seen a man naked before.

Gray reaches out and pulls me toward him. He grips the edges of my pants and pulls them all the way down, surprising me when my panties go with them. Now, I am completely bare in front of him. I hear a deep groan in the back of his throat. He quickly removes his boxers, the only piece of fabric between the two of us, and before I even get a chance to look down, he pulls us both into the steamy water.

The combination of my lust and the steam makes it hard to see straight. I feel Gray's hard body behind me and I let my head fall back with a gasp. The hot water on my skin and Gray's warm hands exploring my body are almost too much to handle. He grips my hips and turns me around fast, so I'm facing him. The movement makes me dizzy, and I grab onto his wet body. He stares right into my eyes before he crashes his lips to mine and devours me. His tongue pushes into my mouth and I moan. I can feel him hard between us and I feel a warm heat travel low in my body. His hands travel down, ever so slowly, barely touching. I feel each fingertip as it runs down from my shoulder, outlining my outer boob, moving down my navel, until he reaches my core. And then he stops. He stops moving, and he stops kissing me, looking right into my eyes again.

"I want to hear you scream my name, Charlie." His husky words repeat in my head over and over as he moves his hand lower and everything around me but Gray disappears.

CHAPTER 15

Gray

We are lying in my bed, Charlie curled up in a ball sleeping, while my body spoons hers possessively. I never want this afternoon to end. She is magnificent. I want to explore her body for the rest of the day. But, I know I can't. I have too much on the line to lay here and ravage her body for the next 24 hours. Instead, I know I have to bring up a dreadful topic to my girl. Time to wake her up.

Putting my hand on her shoulder, I gently rock her until she moans and shifts. *Shit... Don't think about that moan. Stay focused.*

"Sweetheart, wake up. I wanna talk to you," I say the words softly into her ear, and finally, her beautiful blue eyes blink open until she is smiling up at me.

"I love waking up next to you." Her voice is coated in sleep, making her sound a bit gravely and so damn sexy. "What's up?" She starts to sit up, pulling the sheet around her still naked body. We didn't go all the way, as much as we both wanted to. I didn't want to rush it, knowing it was her first time. I wanted to make her first time special, with no danger looming over either of us.

"Would you be willing to tell me about your past?" The words sound harsh as they pass my lips and I curse myself for asking it.

She blinks a few times before looking up at me. Her smile fades slightly, but it's still present. She thinks about it for a moment before a look of determination comes over her. "Normally, I would have shut down at the mere thought of speaking to anyone about my past. But, I want you to know everything about me. I want to let you in. So, yes. I'll tell you." I kiss her hand as she takes a deep breath.

"I was born in New Hampshire, in a really small town called Bridgeport. I'm an only child, but my parents made sure I never felt like I was missing out. They were the best parents a kid could ask for. They made every birthday extravagant, every holiday a fairytale, every thunderstorm a game..." Her words cut out as she swallows. "I was seven years old when it happened. It was a particularly bad thunderstorm, and I ran to my parent's room because I was scared. We were lying in their bed, playing a game to keep my mind off the storm, when we heard a loud crash downstairs. I remember the sound so clearly." She closes her eyes and I watch her lip quiver slightly. "Anyway, my dad told us to stay upstairs while he went to check it out. It was so quiet in the house once he walked out of the room, besides the occasional crack of thunder. And then, I heard voices. Voices that didn't sound like my dad's. I heard him yell and a really loud sound that made my ears ring. I know now that it was a gunshot." She stares ahead as a single tear falls from her eyes.

"My mom screamed when she heard the noise and ran with me in her arms to put me in her closet. I begged her to come in with me, to hold me and play the game until dad came back up. But she just grabbed my face and kissed my forehead before telling me she loved me more than anything. That was the last time I saw her face. The last time I heard either of their voices. I didn't say it back. I never got to tell them how much I love them." Her voice shakes from the pain and I feel tears in my eyes but don't let them fall in front of her. "I laid in the black, dark closet for what felt like hours, days maybe. And then, I heard footsteps outside the door. I thought it was my mom and dad. I was so happy they were back. So, I opened the door, and it all went black. I have no memory of what happened after that... Until, I woke up in a dirty cold cell, with two men next to me." My heart stops beating at her words. I don't think I'm ready to hear this.

"I remember hearing them talk about me getting shipped off on some private plane, but it's all a little foggy. They kept me with them for a month. I spent the month with barely enough food to survive. Each day I wished that was the day I would finally die, but I never did. They would grab at my body, and kiss and bite me. If I ever screamed or cried, they would beat me. They would cut me with their pocket knives for fun." She sniffles as the memories consume her and I grab her hand. I don't realize I'm shaking with anger until I'm holding onto her. "There was this man who was always talking on the phone, I forget his name. He told them they could do whatever they wanted with me, but I had to remain a virgin or I wouldn't be worth as much. I remember wondering what a virgin was... I was so young..." She tries to hold herself together, staring at the bare wall of my bedroom, while I'm over here a shaky, rage filled beast. I want to burn the entire world until there is nothing left but us. But, she sits here so strong and collected as she relives every horrible memory she ever went through.

"How did you get away?"

She laughs but it sounds empty. "I didn't miraculously become this strong willed girl who figured out how to escape if that's what you're thinking." She swallows hard again, voice shaking and barely a whisper. "We were in the car at the end of the month, on our way to the plane they kept speaking about. I was barely able to walk from the malnutrition and my injuries. They tied me up and blindfolded me, throwing me in the back of their car. I remember driving for a while, and then suddenly the car tires were screeching and the two hooded men were screaming at someone. I heard the sound of hands hitting flesh really hard, and then two of those loud ringing noises that I didn't realize were gunshots, and then silence. I waited in the back of the car, terrified of what was about to happen. I heard the trunk door open and I could see light through the blindfold. There were two voices talking, a man and a woman, but I couldn't make out what they were saying. Then, the man picked me up and the woman took the blindfold and rope off. I remember looking over at the woman and thinking she was the most beautiful person in the world. She had this black curly long hair that flew around her face in the wind and her eyes were so big and blue. Your eyes are actually really similar in color to hers, come to think of it." She laughs at this realization, but my heart is beating out of my chest. "She reminded me of my mom. They brought me over to a police station, but refused to come in with me, telling me they had to go and take care of their own babies. The woman cried when she left me, and she hugged me for a long time telling me everything would be okay now. I have never and will never forget them. They saved me from hell, and I never got to thank them before they left me." She stops talking. I feel like I can't breathe. I am overwhelmed by everything she just told me and all I want to do is grab her and hold on tight. But, there is something specific she said that keeps ringing in my ears. The man and woman that saved her. The way she described the woman, how she had my eyes. She had *her* hair. It seemed like too much of a coincidence, but there was no way it was them.

"Sweetheart, do you remember the names of the people that saved you?" My heart was in my throat as I waited for her to answer. It couldn't be, there's no way.

"Yeah. Their names were Alex and Matilda, but she told me to call her-"

"Tilly." I interrupt her without meaning to. I can no longer hear her talking as my mind tries to process the information. I can see her lips moving, talking to me, as her brows furrow in confusion, but I can't hear any of the words. I can barely even see her. I try to stand up and stumble backwards, making my way to the front door. I don't care that I'm only wearing a pair of sweatpants. I don't comprehend the sound of Charlie calling after me. All I can hear are their names.

Their names. The names I have mourned for years. Alex and Tilly.

My mom and dad.

CHAPTER 16

Charlie

I'm yelling after Gray as he stumbles away from me. He has a haunted look in his eyes and I have no idea what caused it. He knew Tilly's name, which confused the hell out of me, but now I just want to make sure he's okay. He is out the door before I can even get his shirt over my head to conceal my naked body. I run after him, yelling his name, but his truck takes off onto the road.

"Fuck." I feel adrenaline running through my body. It's from the fear of Gray running from me, but also from the empowering feeling of finally telling my story. The words wouldn't stop once they started, and I am so happy I told him. Well, I was, until he shut down and ran from me. What could have caused that kind of reaction? He was fine until I mentioned those two names.

Walking back into the house I go back into his room to put my own clothes on. I have my jeans and my bra on when I hear a phone ringing on the bed. Searching through the covers, I find Gray's phone and look at the screen. The name Richard flashes across it and I feel like I know that name from somewhere. I decide to answer it, in case it's important.

I press the answer button and before I can say hello someone talks on the other line.

"You're running out of time Grayson. Ronny and Jacob just told me you ran out on her? Not the way to-" His words fade out as the sound of my racing heart takes its place. How did I not recognize his voice before? Richard. The mayor. The name of the faceless man on the phone from my childhood. The man that wanted to use me to make him money. The man who broke me. His voice from years ago plays through my head as I drop the phone to the ground.

"You boys can do whatever you want to her, just don't fuck her. That's reserved for Antonio. He is paying a lot of money to make sure she is a virgin."

I hear the front door open and close as I try to bring myself back. My body is shaking from finding out the mayor had something to do with my nightmares as I walk out of the bedroom still in my bra. I look for Gray, but what I find sends ice through my entire body. I try to blink, hoping they will disappear. That they are just another figment of my imagination. That they are just the men on the back of my eyelids, unable to actually get to me. Except, when I blink, they get closer. Their hoods are up, but with their next step, they remove them and reveal their blonde hair and bald head. They stare at me, their dark beady eyes looking all over my body. The bald man licks his lips as they stalk towards me. I'm frozen in place. Frozen to the floor from the ice that has consumed my entire body. I can't breathe, can't blink, can't scream, or cry, or flail. Nothing. I can barely hear the words that leave their mouths.

"Fuck, pretty girl, you knew we were coming didn't you?" The bald man stops less than a foot in front of me.

"We've missed you and that little mouth of yours. You've gotten sexier, huh?" Jacob, the other man, comes up and whispers in my ear. "You can still call me daddy. I have been wanting to hear that pretty mouth of yours call me daddy again." He pushes his lower half up against my body.

No no no. This can't be happening. Move Charlotte... MOVE! But

Charlotte doesn't answer. She doesn't move or whimper or cry. She sits in the dark, like she always does.

I hate myself for shutting down during a time I should be kicking and fighting. But, instead, I'm hiding away in the back of my mind, begging for the videos playing through my eyes to shut off. I watch the video from the safety of my dark mind. I watch as the bald man, Ronny, grabs my arms and puts them behind me. I watch as Jacob licks the side of my face before putting tape over my mouth. And I watch as a needle enters the side of my neck, until finally... finally... The videos stop playing and I'm surrounded by the peaceful darkness.

CHAPTER 17

Gray

I 'm driving down the road, no idea where I'm going. I check the clock on my dashboard and see I've been driving for twenty minutes. It felt like two. The stories Charlie told me replay in my mind. Her parents dying. The men torturing her. The man who bought her. My parents saving her. How is it possible that they saved her... that she met them? I feel tears falling down my cheeks as I picture my parents taking care of the girl I love. The girl who needs protecting after everything she went through. Realization hits me. *Fuck.*

I should be protecting her, but instead, I ran because of my own overwhelming feelings. She poured her entire past out to me, every horrible detail, and what did I do? I ran. She is probably crying in my bed, all alone, reliving everything that happened when she was younger.

Spinning my truck around I push the gas pedal to the floor and make my way back to the house. When I pull up to the curb, I barely manage to get the truck into park before jumping out.

I notice the front door to my house is open. Running inside, I call Charlie's name.

"Charlie, baby, I'm so sorry. I didn't mean to run." I am calling out into the still air. Walking into my bedroom I look around and come up short. She must have gone home. I throw my shirt on quickly and then turn around to leave when I notice her white tank top and black sweater on the floor. Why wouldn't she put all of her clothes back on? I see my phone on the ground and pick it up. I go straight to my call log, to click on Charlie's name, and notice a phone call with Richard from forty minutes ago. A phone call that was answered and lasted two minutes. My stomach flips upside down. What did Richard say to Charlie? Why did she leave?

Walking out of the room, my eyes spot something on the floor in front of me. I bend down and pick up the small syringe that has clearly been emptied. My entire body goes numb. *No.*

Please God no.

Running out of the house I sprint to Charlies. Without knocking, I throw the door open and start screaming her name through the house. Her uncle comes running down the stairs.

"What the fuck do you think you're doing Grayson?" He comes up to me, trying to be intimidating.

"Brian, where is Charlie? Have you seen Charlie?" The words are coming out so fast I doubt he can understand me.

"She was supposed to be with you. Where is she?" I hear the change in his tone as panic starts to set in.

"She's gone Brian. You don't understand. She's not safe. Do you have any idea what you did bringing her here?" I am screaming by the time I finish my sentence.

"What the fuck are you talking about?" he screams back at me.

"The scholarship... The one Charlie got to Pleasant Grove... It was a set up... The men who took her, the man behind it all...they set you up so she would be right where he needed her. And now she's gone again! They have her Brian." I feel the tears falling from my eyes as I look at her uncle. His face is full of panic and fear.

"What do we do? Grayson, how do you know this? What do we do? We have to get her back. I can't lose her. Please, I can't lose her too." He falls to his knees and covers his face with his hands as he cries. I feel bad for the guy, but I need to focus on getting Charlie back, for the both of us.

"I will get her back Brian, I promise." The words leave my mouth as I head out the front door and run to my truck. I take out my phone and click Richard's name.

"What do you want?" His voice spits through the phone.

"Where is she, Richard? I swear to God. Where the fuck is she?"

"Ava? She's still safe in Spain, for now." He chuckles at the other end of the phone.

"No! Charlotte. Where is Charlotte? I know you took her." I'm yelling into the phone as I put my truck in drive. The other line goes silent for a second and I am about to scream at him again when he finally answers.

"I don't have her, Grayson. Ronny and Jacob must have interfered. Those mother fuckers. I told them not to interfere. They fucked it up the first time!" *The first time.* These are the same sick fucks that tortured Charlie the first time. My chest squeezes at the thought of Charlie alone with them again. I need to find her.

"Where would they have brought her? Tell me, God dammit!"

"Fuck. Let me find their location." His voice comes through the phone. I wait for him to speak again. "They are heading towards New Hampshire. Those idiots are probably bringing her to the same spot they had her the first time. It's an abandoned jail in a run-down town in New Hampshire. It will take you at least two hours to get there." He stops talking. "They want revenge, Grayson. They were both shot because of her. You better hope you get to her before they fucking kill her. If she's dead, Ava might as well be dead too. I'll send the address." With that he hangs up.

I speed down the highway, waiting for the message with the address to come through. I program it into my GPS, and the woman in the box announces it will take two hours and nine minutes to get there. I press the pedal down, determined to get there in half the time.

I'm coming, sweetheart, just hold on.

CHAPTER 18

Charlie

My eyes slowly open up, everything around me is blurry. I must still be in Gray's bed. I was exhausted after our shower. God, he made my entire body feel so good. I've never experienced anything so amazing.

My muscles feel sore as I groan, feeling the uncomfortable mattress under my back. Gray needs a new bed; how does he sleep on this thing? I open my eyes and blink a few times, willing the fog from my deep sleep to dissipate. My breath catches in my throat.

I'm not in Gray's room. I'm in the cell. The cell from my nightmares. The cell that I have spent so much of my life in. I look around and see the same toilet sitting next to the small bed I am lying on. It's covered in mold and slime, making my stomach flip. The concrete floor is barely visible under the dirt and garbage. The light above me swings, squeaking with each movement. I close my eyes again, wanting to wake up from this nightmare. *Come on, Charlie. Wake up!* I throw my head back, hitting it off the metal bed frame to try to wake up, but the scene before me doesn't change. I hiss from the pain. That's when I hear a laugh and everything comes back to me. Gray leaving. The mayor calling. Ronny and Jacob... No... I look in the corner where the laugh came from and see them both sitting there watching me.

"You still like pain don't you Charlotte?" Ronny isn't looking at my face, but instead at my body. It's that moment I realize I'm not wearing a shirt still and my jeans are now lying on the floor next to the bed. I look down and see the black bra and panties I still have on. I try to reach down to cover my body, but my hands are stuck where they are. I look up and see that they are tied to either side of the bed frame. Panic starts to take over as I flail and cry.

"Please, don't do this. You don't have to do this. Please." I'm begging them both, with tears in my eyes.

"Keep begging." I can see the desire in both of their eyes from across the room. Jacob reaches down and puts his hands near the front of his pants, moving it up and down as he moans. *This can't be happening.* I close my eyes tightly and beg for the blackness to consume me again. Take me away from this moment. But, when I open them back up, I'm still on this bed in the cold cell. Ronny is standing now and my heart beat speeds up. He slowly walks my way, as I hear Jacob unzip his pants in the corner. My body is flailing against the restraints on my hands. I am pulling against them so hard, they bite into my skin, drawing blood and making the air smell of copper.

"It's been too long, pretty girl. We have been waiting for the day that we would be able to see you again." He pulls his shirt over his head and reveals a long scar across his chest. "Because of you, we were both shot and left for dead. I had to have open heart surgery. Spent 6 months in a coma in the ICU." He looks angry now, his nostrils flaring as he looks down at me.

"I'm sorry, I'm so sorry. I didn't mean it. I didn't know they were coming. Please, I had-" A sharp slap across my face silences me and makes my ears ring.

"Don't you dare interrupt me! You clearly lost your manners since leaving us." He bends down and looks me right in my tear filled eyes. "Guess what, pretty girl? We took you for ourselves this time, and we get to do whatever we want with you until I squeeze that pretty little neck of yours and steal your last breath." He chuckles low as his rough hand glides up my leg, over my stomach and lands on my chest. He stops there and squeezes my breast in a vice-like grip, making me cry out in pain. The kick to my ribs from his steel toe boot that comes next steals the air from my lungs, preventing me from screaming.

"You know I hate when you scream." He is spitting on my body as he talks. I can barely comprehend what's happening through the pain at my side. I can't take a full breath, and the lack of oxygen is making my lungs burn.

"Why-" I try to breathe through the burn in my lungs. "Why are you-" I can't finish the sentence.

"Why are we doing this?" He laughs. "Well, it started off as a simple job. Our boss, Richard Whitlock, is one of the most powerful men in this damn country. Your stupid fucking father pissed him off and boom, mommy and daddy are dead. But, that leaves their perfect little daughter. Such a waste to put a bullet between her eyes too." I sob, already knowing this story, as his hand comes out and rubs my face. "So, he sold you off. Made lots of money on the brown haired, blue eyed, virgin. Apparently people in Europe pay big money for little Americans like you. We were supposed to deliver you then. Now? We couldn't keep away. Why should some prick in Europe get to enjoy what is rightfully ours? We taught you so well back then. Spent so much time with that pretty little face of yours. So, we decided if anyone should get you, it's us. We get to fuck you when we want to. Hit you when we want to." He rubs his fingers over my stomach, tracing the scars and making them feel like they are being ripped open all over again. "Mmmm, cut you when we want to. You belong to us. Never forget that. You will always belong to us, and I'm going to make sure everyone knows that." He looks over at Jacob and nods his head. Jacob stops what he's doing and throws something our way. Ronny catches it and the sound of a blade flipping open hits my ears. It might as well be a gunshot; the noise is so loud in my head.

I watch, unable to scream as Ronny swings one leg around the bed and straddles my body. He is on top of my legs, holding them in place. I can no longer move, simply watch in fear. Ronny takes the knife and brings it to his mouth, licking the sharp metal before bringing it down to my abdomen. His hand is positioned over the ribs he just kicked, and I know what's about to come is going to make the pain a lot worse.

I feel the first initial contact of the knife and the sharp sting takes my breath away. I grit my teeth and try not to scream, knowing that will only make this worse. He pushes hard and deep, letting the blade carve into my flesh. My eyes are squeezed as tight as they can go and I'm holding my breath, waiting for the slicing to stop. He keeps picking his hand up for a second and then going back down in another spot. After what feels like an hour, he pulls his hand away, leans back and looks at his work. His face lights up in a sick smile.

"Oh baby, now you're mine forever." I can feel how turned on he is as he looks down at my torn up abdomen. I can feel the blood dripping down my ribs onto the bed and the smell of copper is stronger than before. I pray that was the worst of it, but my prayers go unnoticed as Ronny shifts higher up on my body. His legs are now wrapped around my stomach, where I can feel his hard on digging into me.

Ronny leans forward, rubbing against my fresh wounds with his leg, and his face comes into view. He suddenly slams his face hard against mine, crashing his lips to my own. He smells like cigarettes and stale beer, the smell makes my stomach roll, threatening to spill its contents. He shoves his tongue into my mouth and I try to pull away but I'm trapped where I am. He bites down hard on my lip and blood pools into my mouth, running down my throat and making me choke. I try to hold it in, but my body refuses. I cough, trying to get the blood out of my lungs and end up spitting it onto Ronny's face.

"You fucking bitch." His fist hits my cheek hard and fast. I can barely feel the sharp pain at this point. He wipes his face with his arm and grabs something from his back pocket. Fear consumes me as I wait for the next slice of his knife to hit my face too, but instead he places a dirty rag into my mouth, making me gag. I try to scream but it's now muffled by the fabric. Once the gag is in place, Ronny moves off of me and stands back up.

"I bet you're still a virgin aren't you, pretty girl? You were saving yourself for us, huh?" He pushes himself against my side, rubbing against my hip. "I'm going to fuck you so hard, that gag in your mouth won't be able to hide your screams."

"I can't decide if I want to remove the rag and fuck her pretty little mouth at the same time or wait my turn." Jacob's words come from the corner and they both laugh. I only sob harder.

I watch as Ronny slowly moves down to the opposite end of the bed. He is staring at my body again and his tongue snakes out and licks his lips. From my peripheral vision I see Jacob stand and walk closer, still moving his hand up and down where his pants used to be. I am frozen here, begging for something to take me from this moment. To remove me from my own body so I don't have to live through this. Please God, just kill me now.

Instead, I feel Ronny's dirty hands grip my underwear as he pulls them down past my thighs. I hear his deep growl as he looks over my body. I see Jacob coming up to where my head is, standing over me as he groans. I feel the tears falling faster down my cheeks, knowing what's about to happen will ruin me forever. Ronny's hands start to push my legs open and I close my eyes tight, trying to take myself from this moment by picturing something happy. I picture my mom and dad holding me, rocking me back and forth as they sing to me. I picture Tilly's beautiful hair flying in the wind as she hugs me goodbye and kisses my cheek. I picture Uncle Brian sitting on the couch with me, pretending he isn't crying, as we watch sappy romance movies. I picture Paxton teasing me and making stupid jokes. And then

I picture Grayson. I picture his beautiful blue eyes staring into mine. I picture his mouth, curving up into a smile before his laugh hits my ears. I picture him whispering the words I love you.

I hear flesh hitting flesh and refuse to open my eyes, letting the pictures in my head take me away. I hear a body hit the floor and then the sound of bones cracking hits my ears. Ronny curses, and then grunts loudly before there is silence. I can't open my eyes, scared to see what will be on the other side of the darkness. I feel a hand on my arm, as the gag is removed from my mouth. Someone is calling my name, but it sounds so distant. I feel my head shaking back and forth violently, but I can't stop it. The voice keeps calling my name, until finally I hear a strained "sweetheart." My eyes shoot open at their own accord and search for him.

In front of me, Gray is kneeling near the bed, tears falling from his eyes. I whimper, knowing he is only a figment of my imagination and he's not actually here. I try to blink him away, but he doesn't fade. He just stares at me, all puffy eyed.

"Gray?" My voice comes out in a hoarse whisper. He sighs heavily and looks down at the bed, whispering something. I hear him say the words "thank you God" over and over again. He looks back up at me and reaches for the ties around my hands. He fumbles to get them off and I wince at the pain as they dig into the fresh wounds.

"I'm sorry, sweetheart, I'm so sorry." He pulls them off of me and I try to sit up to hug him, but the pain in my rib makes me scream out. "Shit, I think your ribs are broken. Don't move too much, it will only hurt more." He stands before bending down and picking me up into his arms. I let my head rest on his chest, listening to his racing heart beat as he carries me out of this hell. I pray this isn't all in my head. I pray I'm not lying on the dirty mattress still, with Ronny between my legs taking the last innocence I have.

"Please be real. Please be real," I whisper the words through my sobs.

"I'm real sweetheart, you're safe. I'm here. I'll never let you go." Gray whispers into my ear as we walk out of the building that has housed so many of my nightmares. I feel every step he takes, every beat of his heart, every breath that escapes his lungs. The air is chilly and I can smell the ocean. *Where are we?* I realize I never figured out where the prison that has haunted me for so long even was. I could be in California for all I know.

"Where are we?" I barely get the words out, the pain in my ribs intensifies every time I talk.

"New Hampshire." The words come out clipped. I was born in this state. The last time I knew I was here, I was with my parents. I was laughing and smiling and playing games. I was running around chasing my dad as he pretended to be scared. I was cooking with my mom in the house I grew up in. The memories hit me hard. I never wanted to come back, especially not like this.

I curl up into Gray's chest, trying to ignore everything around me, everything in my mind, and focus on his beating heart. I hear Gray's truck beep in the distance as he unlocks it. He shifts to open the door and then carefully places me lying down in the back seat. The movement makes my ribs burn. It feels like there is a knife inside my body that is desperately trying to break it's way free.

"You need to go to the hospital, sweetheart." I barely hear his voice. He sounds far away.

"No, I hate hospitals." Memories of being in the hospital after the incident come rushing back. The loud beeping. The fluorescent lights. The doctors coming in and out, talking to each other like I wasn't there. They stuck me with so many needles, drawing what seemed like buckets of blood. Made me get undressed just like *they* did and checked my whole body. "I'll be with you the whole time. It will be okay."

"You promise?" The words come out breathy and I doubt he even heard them.

"I promise, sweetheart. I promise."

CHAPTER 19

Gray

I jump into the front seat and try to calm my racing heart. The images of Charlie lying on that bed... Those fuckers getting ready to... God, I couldn't even think the words in my mind. The minute I walked into that abandoned jail and saw them standing over her, pulling her legs apart and jacking off near her head. I swear I saw black. I don't remember hitting them. I can still hear the sound of their bones breaking under my fist, and the proof is all over my bruised hands, but all I see is black when I try to remember it.

After I knocked them both out, I looked down at Charlie and a part of me broke. A part of me that will never heal. The tears streaming down her bruised cheeks, the gag in her mouth, her eyes squeezed shut in fear. And her ribs... The bruising was a messy swirl of purples, blues, and greens. The cuts on top of it made my stomach want to empty its contents. The bright red lines were carved into her soft skin, with blood still escaping from them. *Ronny.* The fucker cut his name into my Charlie. His name will forever be etched into her already scarred body. I wanted to cry for her. To prevent her from ever seeing the awful word. But, I knew she would see it eventually. And I will be there to hold her when she does.

I drive to the nearest hospital after I search for one on my phone. It is only fifteen minutes away, but it feels like hours before I pull into the emergency entrance. I remove my shirt and slip the neck around Charlie's head, until her abdomen is covered. I don't bother putting her arms in the holes, for her sake. I grab her in my arms again and kiss the top of her head. I jog through the emergency room doors and go straight to the first person I see. She is a receptionist behind a desk, meant to check people in.

"Please, you need to help her. I think her ribs are broken." My voice startles the woman and she looks up. Once her eyes land on Charlie in my arms, concern covers her face. She grabs the phone in front of her and two seconds later there are two nurses coming from the double doors in front of me, wheeling a bed toward us. They help me get her on the bed and I start to follow.

"Are you family?" The one nurse asks me before we get to the emergency room doors.

"I'm her boyfriend." I regret saying the words the minute they leave my mouth. I should have just said yes.

"I'm sorry, you need to stay out in the waiting room." Before I can respond they rush through the doors and they close automatically behind them. I am left standing alone in the empty waiting room. The receptionist calls me over and hands me a scrub shirt, reminding me that I'm shirtless. I throw it on and look around, finding the chair closest to the emergency room doors and sitting down. The severity of what could have been hits me again. If I was even a minute later... That fucker would have destroyed her forever.

Remembering that I grabbed Charlie's phone from my room before I ran out, I reach for it in my pocket and go to her messages. I need to let Brian know that she's with me, that she's safe... at least for now. I see there are two new messages, one from Brian, and one from Paxton. I tell myself not to look. Not to pry. But my fingers move before I can stop them and I click on his name.

Paxton: Charlie girl, I'm sorry. I'm sorry for everything. I'm sorry for trying to kiss you again after what happened the first time. I'm sorry for getting angry when you told me you were with him. I'm sorry for telling you to leave. I care about you so much, I just got angry when I found out you were with someone else. Especially who you're with. You need to be careful, Charlie. I don't want you to get hurt. You're my best friend and I miss you like crazy. Can I come see you, please? I can pick you up and we can go get some ice cream :)

So many thoughts circle through my head after reading his message. He is the one that bit Charlie's lip when I first met her. That mother fucker. Clearly she told Paxton about me, so did he tell her we were technically brothers? What does Charlie know? And the thought that overpowers all of the others. Does Paxton not know where she is right now? How could he not know? He was the biggest suck up to his father. He defended everything that his father has ever done. I figured he was involved with every deal Richard had going. I figured he was helping his father get to Charlie, and that was the only reason they were friends. He could very well be pretending with that message, but what's the point of sending that after she was already taken?

Before I do something stupid, like text him off her phone to find out, I go over to Brian's name and type a short message.

Me: This is Gray. We are at a hospital in New Hampshire. She's alright, probably just a broken rib. You can come if you want, but we will probably be discharged and headed back home by the time you get out here. We will call you on the way back to Vermont.

Brian: Hospital??? What happened to her? Grayson I'm freaking out over here. I need some answers. Who took her?

Me: The same fuckers that took her the first time.

I wait for an answer but after a few minutes of silence, I slip the phone back into my pocket. I slouch down in the chair a bit, try to clear my mind of everything that happened, and wait.

CHAPTER 20

Charlie

"**F**ollow my pen with your eyes." The older woman named Dr. Green instructs. I trace the pattern her pen makes in the air with my eyes. "Good. Your face and wrists look nasty, but they will heal soon, so the only concern is your ribs. You have a fractured rib, but luckily it didn't puncture your lungs or any other vital organs. It's a small fracture, so it shouldn't take too long to heal. But it will hurt for a while when you touch it or take a deep breath... The nurse will explain what you need to do when you leave here, and she will give you printed instructions."

"Thank you so much." The words come out strained. I expect her to leave, but she lingers, staring at me.

"Charlotte. We need to discuss what happened here. Have you looked at your ribs?" Her question throws me. I don't need to look at my ribs to know they are pretty messed up.

"No, what do you mean?" As I'm talking she stands up and goes into the cabinet near the sink. She grabs a small circle mirror and walks towards me.

"Don't bend over, it will hurt. Just take a look in the mirror for me Ms. Briar." I take in her words and my eyebrows furrow in confusion. That is, until I look into the mirror. The bruising is dark purple and green, covering half of my abdomen, but that's not what I'm staring at. That's not what brings tears to my eyes and makes me want to scream. Bright red letters are covering my ribs. In the mirror they are backwards, but I know what they say. Ronny. He carved his name into my skin, marking me forever. Marking me worse than I already was.

"That man who brought you in here. That's your boyfriend?" I can only nod my head yes as I stare at my marred skin. "Charlotte, I know it's hard to admit, especially to a stranger, but if he did this to you, you need to tell me. For your safety. Is that Ronny?" Her question makes me tear my eyes off the mirror and look right at her.

"What? No. He saved me from them. He saved my life."

"Them?" She won't stop staring at me. "Okay, hold on Charlotte. I had the nurse call the police when you came in. There is an officer outside in the hall and he is going to want to hear what happened." She walks out the door and then returns with a male police officer behind her. He is probably in his late 30's. His hair has a few grays scattered throughout, and his face is set in a serious expression.

"Hi Charlotte. I'm Officer Bennet." He takes a seat in front of me and Dr. Green stands near the door. "Can you tell me everything you remember?" I realize just then that I actually know who did this. Before, all I had was the first names of the assholes who tortured me.

Before, I was too small and scared to speak up. Before, I was alone. But, now? I have Grayson. I have Uncle Brian. I can do this.

"Their names are Ronny and Jacob. I don't know their last names. But I know who hired them. This is the second time they have done this to me. The first time I was eight. They got away with it but I can't let them this time. They were hired by a man named Richard Whitlock. He's the one behind all of this." I'm talking so fast I forget to breathe between sentences. I'm about to keep going when I see Officer Bennet stand up, his eyes avoiding my face at all costs.

"Where are you going? I haven't finished-"

"Yes, you have Miss. Briar. It's time for me to go." He doesn't look me in the eyes. He doesn't say goodbye. He just turns around and walks out of the room. I look at Dr. Green and feel a bit of relief when she looks just as confused as I am. She looks angry as well. She puts her finger up, to signal for me to wait a minute, and then walks out after the officer.

I sit in the uncomfortable bed, trying to think of anything but what I just went through. The word etched on my skin burns, constantly reminding me of his hands on my body. I feel a bit of hope at the thought that they may all finally get what they deserve. They have to at least question Richard, right? Gray can vouch for me, he saw Ronny and Jacob. He beat them up. We can show them where they took me. If they question them, I'm sure they will give Richard up. They will all finally rot in jail. That thought brings a smile to my face, as sick as that may sound.

I wait for Dr. Green to return, but she never does. It's at least an hour and a half before someone finally comes into my room. She's a pretty nurse. Blonde hair in a tight ponytail, brown eyes that sparkle when she smiles. She comes in and grabs some supplies from the cabinet before walking toward me.

"Alright Charlotte, time for you to get out of this place! I'm going to remove your IV and then we will go over your discharge instructions before your uncle comes and gets you." She sits next to me and I put my arm out for her to reach.

"My uncle is here?" The thought of seeing him makes me want to cry. I needed him. I needed his hugs. I needed his horrible jokes and his singing. I couldn't wait to see him.

"Yes! He arrived about 10 minutes ago." The nurse, Stacy, smiles down at me.

"Is Gray with him? The man that brought me to the emergency room."

"I wasn't aware that someone else brought you here. He is probably still in the ER waiting room. After I finish up here, I will go find him myself and meet you and your uncle at the main entrance."

"Thank you so much." I smile at her and relax in my bed. She removes the IV with one swift movement and places a gauze and tape over the small needle hole. She tells me what I have to do in order for my ribs to heal. Normal things like rest, ice, how to prevent pneumonia, etc. Then she hands me a packet of paperwork that includes a prescription for pain meds, and has me sign a discharge paper. She places a pair of green scrubs on the bed and stands.

"Alright honey. You change into these, I'll go grab your friend in the waiting room. Your uncle is waiting outside the room now." I thank her as she leaves before I grab for the shirt and carefully place it over my head. The pain meds they gave me in the IV are helping me with the pain and I can actually move without crying out. I get the shirt on and carefully stand up, with my back to the closed door. I slowly reach down and start to put my legs through the pants, trying not to irritate my ribs. I hear a small squeak, like a door being opened, and quickly glance over and see that the door is closed. Bending over, I grab onto my pants and start to pull them up, moving slowly from the sharp pain radiating from my side.

"Mmmm. Putting on a show for me, Charlotte?" The voice makes the blood in my veins turn to ice. Instead of freezing up, I shoot upright and get my pants situated, hiding myself from his sinister eyes. I turn to face Richard and glare.

"Wh… what are you doing here?" I try not to show how scared I am, but my voice betrays me.

"What do you mean, darling? Why wouldn't your uncle come and get you from the hospital? I'm just doing what's right."

"What are you talking about?" I don't understand what he means. At that moment, Dr. Green walks into the room.

"Alright, you be careful Charlotte. Please take it easy and follow instructions. I have to head to another floor but I'm sure your uncle can handle getting you to the car." She has a smile on her face, but she refuses to look at me. Instead, she looks at the wall, the floor, the fluorescent lights... anything but me.

"Dr. Green. This isn't my uncle. This is the man that kidnapped me. This is the-"

"Please, Char, let's go home now." Richard's voice turns sickeningly sweet and he uses the nickname only my uncle and my parents have ever used for me. The sound of it makes me want to vomit.

Dr. Green doesn't glance my way once before leaving the room, closing the door behind her. Richard's laugh fills the room as I try to run to the door. My injury prevents me from moving fast and Richard beats me there. He blocks the door with his body and looks down at me with a sick smile.

"You think you can turn me into the cops? Think again. I own the fucking cops, no matter what state we are in. I thought that dumb fuck could get the job done, but now I have to intervene." I start to scream but he slaps me across the face and my vision goes blurry. I can barely make anything out in front of me as I hold my cheek, but I feel the familiar sting of a needle entering my skin. My body starts to slouch, but I am still aware of my surroundings. I can feel Richard's slimy hands grab onto me, with a painful grip, as he positions me in front of the wheelchair that was set in the corner of the room earlier. He throws me down into the chair hard, and I try to cry out from the pain, but my mouth doesn't work. I try to talk, but nothing comes out.

I can blink, I can breathe, and I can somewhat move my head. But, besides that, I'm paralyzed.

He opens the door and wheels me out into the hallway. I look at everyone we pass, unable to speak, and all of the workers avoid eye contact. I'm screaming for help in my head, flailing my arms, crying out, but on the outside, I'm completely still. I appear calm and relaxed from whatever drug he injected me with. I remember Stacy saying she would bring Gray to the front and my heart races. He'll save me.

We reach the main entrance and I try to turn my head to look for Gray. I don't see him anywhere. Where is he? I want to scream out his name. I want to cry and beg for help. I want to jump out of this chair and run as fast as I can. I want all of these things to happen right now. But, instead, I am thrown into the back of a car and we drive off into the night.

CHAPTER 21

Gray

"Sir? Sir, wake up." The voice sounds far away. I shift in my sleep, trying to get comfortable. "Sir. Are you with Charlotte Briar?" The voice sounds closer this time and I manage to get my eyes open. My brain feels fuzzy, like I'm waking up after a long night of drinking. Where am I? What happened? I take in my surroundings and everything comes back to me. I'm in the hospital. I'm waiting for Charlie to be discharged. Charlie. Where is she? Is she okay?

I quickly start to stand and regret it when my vision goes blurry and I just about fall to the ground.

"Woah, you okay?" There is a blonde nurse standing in front of me. She puts her hand on my arm and I shove her touch away. I'm not trying to be mean, but I have no interest in this person touching me. Just Charlie.

"Where's Charlie? Is she okay?" My voice is hoarse from my deep sleep. How did I fall asleep? And why do I feel like I've been fucking roofied.

"She's good. She's a strong girl. Her uncle is with her now. He is taking her home. She asked me to come get you." The nurse, her name tag say's Stacy, lets her eyes drag down my body with a shy smile and it takes everything in me not to roll my eyes. I'm not in the mood for this. Wait... did she say her uncle is here? Brian ended up coming? I didn't even tell him the hospital we were at; how did he find us?

"Where are they now?" I ask quickly. I want to see Charlie, something about this situation feels wrong. Brian would have called. He would have told me he was coming. He would have asked where we were.

"They were in her room and I told her we would meet her at the main entrance. I will take you there now." Before she can start walking I rush ahead of her, moving as fast as my groggy body will let me. I follow the signs until I get to the main entrance.

I look around the huge hospital foyer. There are only a few people in the room. One young couple with a baby and then an older man who is doing a crossword. But, no Charlie. Where is she? Maybe she is still in her room? I walk to the front doors and stare out into the dark night. I watch as a black car drives away from the front of the building. Something about it catches my eye. Why does that black Cadillac look so familiar? The realization hits me. That's one of Richard's cars. At that moment I realize exactly where Charlie is. She's in the mother fucking lion's den. And she's about to be slaughtered.

***

How did I let this happen again? How could I have fallen asleep? I don't remember falling asleep. I was sitting in the chair, thinking of Charlie. I was thinking about the first day we met, the way she has opened up to me, how she has changed my life so much already. I was so full of adrenaline from the past few hours that I would never have been able to fall asleep.

That's when it hits me. That fucker must have drugged me. That's the only explanation for me falling asleep the way I did. He must have snuck up and injected me with something like his shit head minions did to Charlie when they took her. I feel my fear and anger creeping up on me. And by creeping, I mean full on slamming into me like a semi-truck. I grab my phone out of my pocket as I jump into my truck and head in the direction I saw his car go.

"Ah, how nice of you to call. I didn't think you'd be awake at this hour." His voice fills my ear and I want to smash my phone.

"Where are you taking her? What the fuck are you playing at here?" I am yelling into the phone.

His sinister laugh flows through the speaker. "This isn't personal. She tried to rat me out to the cops, so I took matters into my own hands. I talked to Antonio and he decided to leave Russia a few days early. I will be keeping her until the drop off tomorrow night. Clearly I can't rely on anyone to get this fucking job done." He stops talking and sighs heavily. "Oh and if you think you're free from this, think again. I'm curious how this little bitch figured out it was me running the show. I'm assuming either you or those dumb fucks told her. Either way, your sister has a one way ticket to the highest bidder now once her trip is over in a few days. Maybe that will teach you not to disobey me." I hear the other line hang up before I can respond. My anger takes over and I find myself screaming as I throw my phone at my windshield. I hear the sound of my phone cracking but I'm too upset to care.

How did I fuck this up so royally? I wanted to save both of them, figure out a way to end Richard before either of them could get hurt. And yet, here I am. Sitting alone in my truck, driving around aimlessly, with both of my girls in danger. I have no way to get to either of them. I don't have a passport to get to Ava, and I have no idea where Richard would take Charlie to hide away for the next two days.

The thought hits me suddenly... I reach into my pocket and grab Charlie's phone.

Clicking the name I have hated for almost ten years.

"Charlie girl?" It sounds like he just woke up. "Are you okay?"

"Paxton, it's Grayson. I need your help." I am short and quick with my words.

"What the fuck are you doing on Charlie's phone? Where is she? Did you fucking hurt her?" He's talking fast and the anger in his voice travels through the phone.

"Did I hurt her? No you dumb ass. Your piece of shit father is taking care of that one."

"What do you mean he's taking care of it?" He sounds genuinely confused.

"He is selling her off to one of his clients overseas, Paxton. He sold her to some sick fuck and now Ava is going to end up God knows where with some other client if I don't save them both."

"Sold her? What does that even mean Grayson? Have you lost your mind?" It hits me then that he doesn't know what I'm talking about.

"Do you have any idea what your father has been doing all of these years? He has been involved in sex trafficking and runs a drug ring. Since I was fourteen he has made me work for him, threatening Ava's life if I refused. He has made me do drug deals, beat up clients, pick up shipments, you name it. But I always refused to work in this part of his world. It's so fucked up and back then as long as Ava was free from it, I pretended it didn't exist. But now he has Charlie." I feel the tears fill both of my eyes. "He has Charlie and he's going to send her off to Portugal with this man who will destroy her. And Ava... Paxton, Ava is so young. Please. I need your help." My sobs make it difficult to get the words out.

"Grayson... I don't understand. I can't believe he would do this. How?" He's in denial but I can hear in his voice that there is a part of him that believes me.

"Please, Paxton. Even if you don't believe it completely, just help me out. Help me find Charlie before..." The words don't come out.

"Alright, how long do we have before this deal is supposed to happen?" I hear him moving around on the other end of the phone.

"Your dad said the guy, Antonio, is coming tomorrow. They are meeting at his private landing strip in New Hampshire. I'm in New Hampshire now."

"Why are you in New Hampshire right now?"

"You seriously don't know anything do you? Charlie was taken from my house earlier today. She was drugged and taken by two fuckers that your father hired. They broke her ribs, cut her with knives, and they were about to." I take a deep breath. "If I didn't get there when I did, they would have raped her." Saying the words out loud tasted bitter in my mouth. The line is quiet for a while.

"Where do I meet you?" His voice is cold and angry.

"Meet me at the Motel 6 off Route 101." With that, he hangs up and I drive like hell.

CHAPTER 22

Charlie

The car comes to a stop after about a half hour. I still can't move, so I haven't been able to sit up to see where we are. I hear Richard get out of the car and then the door near my feet opens up. The air is cold and the salty smell of the ocean hits my nose. His hands grip my legs hard as he yanks me out of the car. My body, unable to catch itself, hits the rough pavement and I barely get the scream to come out from the pain.

"Look who's voice is starting to come back. Just in time." His words make the hair on the back of my neck stand straight up. He bends down to the ground and grabs me around the waist before hauling me over his shoulder, his hands move to my ass and he squeezes tight enough to leave a hand shaped bruise, but I refuse to make a sound. He starts to walk and it takes everything in me to get my head to turn so I can look at my surroundings instead of his backside.

We are surrounded by thick woods, but I can hear the sound of the ocean in the near distance. The waves crashing against the shoreline would almost be relaxing if it wasn't for the fact that I was being held by the devil himself right now. I watch as we step up onto a porch and I hear him open a door. We walk into a large white foyer. The room is filled with expensive coastal decor. I take in each room as we move through them. The foyer leads into an expansive gourmet kitchen with huge windows that overlook what I assume is the ocean. It's too dark to tell.

Richard opens another door and suddenly we are traveling down a set of stairs. The coastal decor continues into the finished basement. There is a huge TV on the wall in front of me along with a pool table and bar. I hear the sound of a keypad being pushed. He enters 6 numbers and then a chime fills the room before the sound of a heavy door opening hits my ears. He walks forward and I just catch the door closing behind us. The hole we walked through slides shut until it disappears and in its place is the bare wall, with no exit.

This room smells different. It smells stale and musty from mildew. The area is dark and the air feels damp on my skin. I don't see any furniture as we walk forward, and suddenly I am being thrown off his shoulder onto the ground. My body hits hard with a thud and I suck in a breath. I blink a few times, waiting for the pain to subside. I take in the room I am in. There is a fluorescent light above us that lights up the almost empty room. There is a small cot to my right and a toilet to my left. I don't notice the worst part at first. I see Richard standing four feet away from me, but separating us is a glass wall. There are four glass walls surrounding me, trapping me in the small prison. I start to hyperventilate. How can I escape one prison just to be put into another? This can't be happening.

"Comfy?" Richard's voice echoes through the glass. I look up at his face to see him smile.

"Wh- why?" The word barely comes out.

"Why? Oh Charlotte. Poor poor Charlotte." He snickers. "You wanna know why? Blame it on your pathetic excuse of a father!"

"My father?" My heart races at his words.

"I went to college with Jack, did you know that? We went to Dartmouth together. He was my best friend. I was studying Political Science and your father was going for Education. We were inseparable. Until your whore of a mother showed up. She was everything to him and I saw less and less of my best friend the closer they got. He focused on her, and I focused on my career goals. The closer he got to Jenny, the closer I got to my Political dreams. Eventually, we went our separate ways. I moved to Vermont and became mayor, and he stayed in New Hampshire and became a pathetic eighth grade math teacher. We both got married, had kids, and our lives just drifted apart." He shakes his head and smirks.

"He kept in touch through the years, but we never got together, until he heard that my father passed. Jack reached out when he heard, and he came to Vermont for the funeral, leaving his perfect little wife and seven year old daughter at home. First time I had seen him in almost eight years.

"You see, Jack didn't know what was going on in my life. With my father passing, his empire suddenly fell on my shoulders. He kept it all a secret, but right before he died, he told me about everything. His connections to the cartel, his relationships with every powerful leader in the world, his many trafficking rings. I was in awe, terrified and disgusted with what he was telling me. That is, until I found out about the money he had coming in. Billions of dollars. Money that he told me would go to me, if I continued with his business. That was the deal. If I took over for him, I would not only get power, but more money than I would know what to do with. How could I say no?" His laugh fills my ears. "But, your father just couldn't stay out of it. He couldn't mind his own fucking business. While he was at the house for the funeral, he walked in on a phone call I had with one of my father's clients. We were having a very heated discussion about how much a specific young lady I was shipping to him was supposed to cost. Jack heard the whole thing.

"He was always the one with the moral compass, just like my fucking brother. They both had to do everything right. Couldn't break any rules, let alone laws. Jack didn't understand. I begged him to drop it. To forget he heard anything. To go back home to his perfect little family and pretend nothing happened. But, he just couldn't fucking let it go. He threatened me. Saying if I didn't stop what I was doing, he would turn me in. My father warned me that loved ones would be against my decisions. He dealt with my brother when he found out. Was able to keep him quiet by threatening his wife and son. So that's what I did. I told Jack if he ever told anyone, I would ruin his precious little family.

"But, your stupid fucking father wanted to 'help me' as he said." He uses air quotes as he speaks. "He tried speaking to my wife, to get her to talk some sense into me. She had no idea about the new life I was living. She wasn't too happy about it. We almost divorced because of it. He tried to ruin my life, so I just returned the favor." He laughs again, loud and maliciously. "One phone call to two little gang members that my father helped out, you know them very well. They were supposed to show up to Jack's house, rough him and his family up a bit, and make sure he never tried anything again. Except, they took it too far. Your father fought too hard. They had to kill him. They shot him right between the eyes, and Jenny just had to come running after her beloved husband. So, she had to go next." The feeling in my legs was coming back as he told the horrible story. I was able to sit up and stare him in the eyes with my own tear filled ones. "They called me telling me what happened. They told me Jack and Jenny Briar were dead, which left their beautiful little girl. I had to be smart. I had to think fast. What do we do with a seven year old girl? We could kill you, but that seemed like a waste. So I had them take you. I had them bring you somewhere no one would find you, and then I called one of my father's customers and told him all about you. I sent him a picture of you and your mother, and he became obsessed. He offered me a million dollars to get you to him. A million dollars for the trashy daughter of a traitorous piece of shit." He spit on the glass as he spoke.

I was sobbing where I sat. Hearing him speak of my parents the way he did. My father was the best man I had ever known. My mother was an angel. Hearing his stories didn't make me feel any different. My dad was just trying to save Richard from a life of crime. He cared about him. And Richard destroyed him. He destroyed everything I ever loved. All because he was greedy for money and power.

"You're a monster. He cared about you. He wanted to help you." I try to magnify my voice, but it comes out quieter than I intended.

"Help me? He was jealous of me. He always was." He fixed his tie and smirked in a proud way. He was disgusting.

"How could you have your best friend killed? How can you live with yourself?" The tears continue to come.

"You think that's bad? I had my brother murdered. I watched it happen. He was the biggest traitor of all. Him and his whore of a wife, Tilly." His words echo in my ears. Killed my brother. Biggest traitor. Tilly.

"Alex and Tilly..." I say the words quietly. "They saved me."

"Yes, and I made sure they would regret going against me. That piece of shit I call my brother got to watch me from wherever he ended up, probably hell if you ask me, as I raised his kids and forced his pathetic excuse of a son into the very same business he hated so much." I look at him in confusion.

"Paxton isn't your real son?" How could Paxton be a part of this business? How could he help him do all of these horrible things?

"What? Of course he is, you idiot. I'm talking about Grayson." My heart stops at the name.

"Gray?" It can't be him. It can't be my Gray. He saved me. I think about the way he always leaves for late night jobs, never once telling me what he does. I think about him telling me his sister lives with their uncle in the rich part of town. I think about the black truck I saw driving down Richard's driveway. The way Paxton reacted when I told him I was with Gray... The way Gray reacted when I talked about Tilly and Alex saving me... No.

"You had no idea, did you? You're new friend Grayson is my

nephew. He does all the dirty work for me with my deals. In fact, you'll never guess who was in charge of getting you on the plane to Portugal this time."

"You're lying. He would never hurt me. He loves me." The last three words barely come out as a whisper.

"Loves you? Oh this just keeps getting better!" His laugh takes over the room, making me jump. "That boy doesn't give a shit about you. He was doing this for a job. He needed you to trust him so he could get you on that plane. He did everything because I told him to. He doesn't care what happens to you. You're just a naive teenager that no one loves. Your parents are dead. Your uncle brought you right to me, knowing I would ship you off. You ruined your uncle's life and he just wants you gone. You have no friends. Face it kid, you have no one left." The tears had dried on my cheeks. There didn't seem to be any more left to fall. He was right. I had no one.

My body slouches forward as his words repeat in my head. Everyone around me was just another devil in disguise. No one cared about what happened to me. I was a burden in everyone's lives. I should have just died all of those years back. I feel everything in my body start to go cold, all at once. The heart that was once racing in my chest goes still. I no longer feel it beating beneath my skin. I no longer feel blood circulating through my body. My fingertips and toes go numb. My lungs don't seem to accept the oxygen that pours into them. My mind begs to shut down. To hide away. To ignore everything around me. To let go of who I am. To let the darkness consume it, until there is nothing left.

CHAPTER 23

Paxton

I walk quickly, checking each room number until I reach room 328. I don't bother knocking as I swing open the door to the shitty Motel 6 room. There are two full beds with gaudy floral bedspreads on them. Gray is sitting on one of them, bent over with his head in his hands. His knee keeps shaking, making his whole body shutter with each movement. I close the door and that seems to get his attention. He jumps and looks up at me. The dark circles under his eyes appear almost purple. It looks like he hasn't eaten in days. His hands are bawled up into tight fists, making the bruises and cuts on his knuckles stand out.

"You look like hell." I walk toward the other bed and sit across from him. The springs in the bed squeak under my weight.

"He has her, Paxton. He has them both." His voice shakes as he speaks. His eyes are puffy and rimmed in red, from crying.

"You need to help me understand, Grayson. I don't know what the fuck to think right now." I have been trying to run through everything he said on the phone on my way here. He said Charlie is in trouble. That my dad is the reason behind it. He said my dad has been running a bunch of crime rings for years.

How could I not have seen it? I remember hearing the strange conversation my dad had in his office. I remember Grayson telling me he hated my father when we were younger. Telling me he was a horrible person, that he wanted to leave with Ava and never come back. I always yelled at him. Told him he should be grateful for what my family has done for him. I had no idea.

"Charlie didn't just show up in Pleasant Grove out of nowhere this year. Your dad tricked her uncle into bringing her to him. He offered to give her a full ride to Pleasant Grove Heights, saying it was a scholarship he gave out to random students across the country. Her Uncle Brian felt he had no choice but to accept it, for Charlie's future. Did Charlie tell you anything about her past?" Grayson was glaring at me.

"No, I could tell something bad had happened to her, but she never actually told me."

"Well, it's not my story to tell. When she is ready, she will tell you. But, all you have to know is that your father had tried to hurt Charlie when she was younger, and he's trying to finish what he started all those years ago. He has a client out in Portugal that is paying for her."

"What do you mean paying for her?" The way he said it made it sound like she was property, not a person.

"Jesus, Paxton, I already explained this. He's involved in sex trafficking. He is getting a shit ton of money for Charlie. This guy, Antonio, will literally own her. Every part of her. She will be forced to do whatever the sick fuck wants. If she disobeys, or tries to escape, a lot of times these types of men just kill them and move on to the next..." Grayson looks down and his voice shakes as he speaks. "I know we don't get along, but I need you. I have been fighting your father alone for seven years. I have been trying to escape him since I was fourteen and he started threatening Ava's life if I didn't work for him. I hate myself for what I have done, but I hate him even more. He's evil Paxton. I thought you knew about it this whole time. I thought you were helping him, keeping his secrets, and letting him threaten Ava. I hated you so much, and I'm sorry for that. I'm sorry for how I treated you. But it was me against the world, with my baby sister on the line. She is everything to me. And now your father is planning on selling her life away. Both of my girls are going to disappear from my life in the next 24 hours if we don't do something." He takes a deep shaky breath as the last few words leave his mouth.

I know it's wrong, but out of everything he said, what sticks out the most is him saying *my girls*. "You really love Charlie, don't you?" He just nods his head yes, keeping his eyes low, as if to hide the pain on his face.

I don't say anything else at first. Trying to sort through all of the information Grayson told me. I never understood why he hated me and my dad. I'd be lying if I said I didn't believe my father was capable of this. He is a master manipulator and black-mailer. I have heard his heated phone calls that he tries to hide. I know he has a dark side, I just didn't know it could be this dark. The thought of him threatening to hurt Ava and Charlie has my blood boiling. "Okay, what do we do?"

His eyes find their way back to mine, swirling with surprise. "You'll help me?"

"Yes. I would do anything for Charlie, I love her too... And the fact that Ava is in danger makes me want to rip my father's head off. She's my sister, Grayson. I'd kill for her." I see a flash of pos-sessiveness take over his face when I start talking, but it's gone so fast I think I imagined it. In its place I see remorse, and maybe even gratitude.

"Your father mentioned the transaction is going to be hap-pening at his private landing strip in New Hampshire. Do you know where that is?"

"Oh, shit. Of course. We had a beach house on the shore that we used to go to all the time before you and Ava moved in with us, it has a landing strip on it right next to the ocean. I figured my dad sold it since we never went back, but that has to be it right?" It seems like the perfect hide away. The house was so private and right on the ocean. There were thick woods surrounding the landing strip as well. I pull my phone out quickly and dial Gina's number. She used to go to the shore with us when we were younger.

"Hello?" Her voice is hoarse from sleep.

"Gina! I need you to tell me the address to the old beach house we used to go to. Do you remember it?"

"Of course I remember it. Why? It's four in the morning Mr. Whitlock."

"It's just for a project, can you give it to me?" I am so thankful for Gina's amazing memory. She rattles off the address and I give her a quick thanks before hanging up. "Alright. I have a feeling this is where Charlie is. What about Ava?"

"She is on a class trip in Spain. Once the trip is over in a few days she is going to be shipped off to another client of his. We need to save Charlie first and then figure out how to get to Ava." He doesn't sound confident as he tells me his plan. Then again, it's not much of a plan at all.

"How are we going to get Charlie away from my dad?"

"That's where you come in. You can distract your dad. He has no idea that you know what he does. You can show up, pretend to be drunk and missing your old childhood beach house or some shit, and distract him enough for me to find Charlie. It could work, right?" He's practically begging for me to agree that his plan will work. He's clearly desperate.

"I mean... maybe? But where would he even keep Charlie? The house is huge."

"I'm going to guess he's keeping her locked up in the basement. Knowing your father he has some sort of security system and dungeon set up there as well." The word dungeon sits in my head and I realize I know exactly where he is keeping Charlie.

"In the basement, the wall to the left of the stairs has a keypad on it. There is a secret room behind that wall. Only my dad and I knew about it. He built it for me when I told him I wanted my own secret lair as a kid. I was obsessed with Batman and was convinced I needed my own bat cave. Even got me a black cape and bat mask." I shake my head, as if the movement will scatter the memories so I can focus. "That has to be where he is keeping her.

You can't get in or out without the code."

"So what's the code?" He is standing already, making his way to the motel room door.

"Fuck. It's a six digit code. It's either his birthday, or my birthday, or maybe my mom's?" I search through my memories for the hundreds of times I pushed the code into the system to get into my lair. I can almost hear the pattern beeping in my mind as my six year old fingers type in the code. "It's my birthday. It's definitely mine. The code is-"

"11-26-02. Let's go. We need to get reinforcements." He walks out of the room and leaves me standing there in awe. After all these years he remembered my birthday? It's definitely not the time to bring it up, so I just shove that thought down deep and run after Gray.

"Reinforcements? What does that mean?"

"Guns. Knives. Anything I may need to get Charlie back." He doesn't look back at me as he answers.

"Where are we going to buy those?" I have never purchased a gun in my life.

"Perks of working for your dad so long? I know a lot of shady people. I know a guy who can get us anything we may need. Just keep your mouth shut and let me do the talking." We make our way into my car without another word. It's time to save Charlie girl.

CHAPTER 24

Charlie

It's been hours since I last saw Richard. I have been sitting on the floor in the same spot since he walked out of the room laughing at me. I can still hear it echoing off the walls. Mocking me and my family. I don't know what time it is, since the room has no windows. For all I know, it's almost time for my transfer. I've come to terms with it. How bad could it be? I know no one is coming for me, and there's no way I can get out of this. I have no one left. If this man wants me, he can have me. But, before long, I'll be dead. Whether I have to disobey him until he kills me, or I get the chance to kill myself first. I'm hoping for the latter. I want to have some control in my own demise.

The thoughts are morbid, but they somehow bring relief to me. I feel calm as I imagine floating in a sea of darkness for the rest of eternity. Or ending up with my parents, wherever they may be. Who knows where I will go, but at this point? Anything is better than here. In the life I live where everyone tricks me. Where no one actually loves me, and I'm just a pawn in a horrible game. If there was a way to kill myself right now, I would. But this room has nothing in it besides a bare bed and a toilet. So, all I can do is wait. Wait until Richard comes back and tells me it's time to go.

My ribs are still on fire. I finally have complete control of my own body, but I haven't taken advantage of that luxury. I don't see a point in getting off this spot on the floor. It will only bring more pain. I picture Ronny's name on my skin and feel bile rise in my throat. My own body isn't even mine anymore. He marked me as his, and pretty soon, this next guy will do the same. He will own me completely. He will take away the last of my innocence. He will strip me of everything I have left. Then again, didn't Gray already do that? He tricked me. Made me fall in love with the idea of this amazing guy, when in reality, he was just doing a job. He wanted to get rid of me, and the only way to get me there was to gain my trust. I remember his hands on my body. His mouth on my mouth. His fingers doing things to me that no one has ever done. He tricked me and I fell hard and fast, desperate for someone to love me. Thinking about him makes the tears fall harder, and I feel a burning sensation on my wrist. I look down and notice his bracelet. The one with a rose surrounded by briars. He told me I was that rose, perfect but hard to get to. That was all bullshit. I'm not a rose. I'm the fucking thorn in everyone's side, my last name is literally Briar. The thought almost makes me laugh.

I hear the sound of the hidden door sliding open and my heart starts to race. That means it's time. That means I'm about to be shipped off to another country with a man who will own me. A man who will use my body, break my mind, crush the little bit of soul I have left. I can already hear my mortality clock ticking, getting closer to my final breath. That couldn't come soon enough. If I could convince Richard to kill me himself, I would. But, why would he kill me if I was going to make him money? Unless I pushed him to his breaking point. Maybe then he would snap. Maybe I could push him so far that he would have no choice but to off me himself. It's a thought that I shove away for later as I watch the figure walk through the hidden door. It's too dark to see his smug face, but I watch him rush to me. He looks frantic in his movements. An automatic light switches on as he approaches, and that's when I see it. His dark messy hair falling onto his forehead. His blue eyes that have watched me break apart in his hands. His worried frown etched on the lips I've kissed countless times. Gray. The man I fell in love with, only to fall even harder into darkness. Darkness he caused. I glare up at him, even though my body instinctively shivers at his presence. I hear the strained whisper leave his lips as he looks down at me.

"Sweetheart."

His voice causes goosebumps to spread across my skin and I hate it. I want to be strong, but I feel like I have no strength left. I turn my eyes away from him, unable to look at his perfect face. "Is it time?" The words are barely a whisper.

"What do you mean?" He sounds confused. "Baby, I came to get you out of here. To save you."

"You put me in here." I'm still not looking at him. How could I? He doesn't talk for a few seconds and I hear his battered breath filling the room.

"I don't know what he told you but I can explain." His voice sounds like it's crumbling.

"That right there is explanation enough. I was a job to you. A way to make money. You used me and made me feel like I could trust you. You made me fall..." I don't finish the sentence, letting the words hang between us. "You got what you wanted. I'm done fighting. I am going willingly." Seeing him again is the last straw that pushes me into submission. Any thoughts I had of fighting or convincing Richard of killing me himself are out the window. All I want is to be on that plane and as far away from these monsters as I can get. Even if I have to be with another monster entirely.

"You're wrong. You are not a job. I didn't use you. You broke me down and made me feel things I never thought I could feel again. Not since my parents died. You made me feel safe. You made me feel hope and trust and love. I've been running for my entire life and you made me feel like I could stop and breathe. Like I wasn't suffocating anymore." His words make me turn to face him. My heart is racing and tears are falling freely down my cheeks. "I fell in love with you the minute I looked into those eyes, sweetheart. I fell in love with the bright light I saw shining through the sad darkness that consumed you. I fell in love with your shyness, but also your witty banter. I fell in love with your touch, your smell, your taste, the sound of your voice. Everything about you.

"This wasn't a job. I had no idea who you were when we met. When Richard told me there was a job I had to take care of, I told him no. I told him I wouldn't do it. I could never hurt you. But, then he threatened my sister. He said if you weren't on the plane, he would sell her off too. She's only thirteen, Charlie. I was never going to let him take you, but I had to pretend I was going along with his plan while I tried to form my own. I had to save you and my sister. But, in the end, I wasn't able to protect either of you. He is a monster and he has had control over me for most of my life. I wanted to protect you, Charlie. Please believe me. You have to believe me." He has almost his entire body pressed up against the glass, like he's trying to get as close to me as possible. I don't know what to think. He sounds so genuine, he has tears falling from his eyes and his voice is strained. Richard was threatening his little sister? She was just a kid. Then again, I was even younger than her when he tried to do this to me the first time.

The first time.... When Tilly and Alex saved me. They were Gray's parents. They died because they saved me. And now Gray was trying to save me and his little sister was going to pay. I couldn't let that happen. I can't let him go through any more pain on my behalf. I won't take his last family member away from him. I was getting on that plane. Whether Gray liked it or not. I look him up and down and notice the gun sticking out of his pants. I need that gun. I start to stand up and move towards him.

"I'm sorry Gray but I'm not coming with you."

"Please, Charlotte, I'm begging you. How do I get this door

open? How do I get you out of here?" He sounds desperate and it tugs at my heart.

"You don't get me out of here. I don't want to go with you. I don't want to be with you." The words feel painful to say, like my body refuses to say the lie. I reach the wall where there is a small slot for food to be thrown in, at least that's what I assume it's for since I haven't been given any since being here. The tears falling from my eyes sting my skin, as if they are acid. I reach my hand into the small opening and reach for Gray. He closes the gap and lets his hand fall into mine. His touch sends electric currents up my arms and I feel more alive than I have since being kidnapped. He drops his head forward and rests it on the glass, closing his eyes. I hear a whispered "please" leave his lips and it nearly breaks me in two. I take this moment to move quickly, reaching for the gun in his pants and when my hands grasp the cold metal I pull it into the room with me.

"What are you doing Charlie?" Grayson jumps back and then his eyes go wide as he sees the gun in my hand. "Baby, what are you doing? Please don't do what I think you are going to do. We can get you out of here. I will take care of you and we can live a long and happy life together. I won't let anything happen to you, please, I love you so much. Don't do this." His voice is shaking so violently and there is a stream of tears rushing down his face. He thinks I'm going to kill myself.

"I'm sorry, Grayson. I'm doing this for you. I love you." I look over at the still open door to the hidden room and ignore Grayson's frantic voice saying my name. "Richard!" The scream isn't as loud as I meant it to be.

"Charlie, what are you doing?" He is pounding on the glass now, but I ignore him.

"RICHARD! RICHARD! COME DOWN QUICK!" I am screaming so loud now that my throat burns. I watch, as all too late, Grayson runs to the door and tries to get it closed with the keypad, but his fingers fumble across the numbers. I hear the sound of footsteps running down the basement stairs. Suddenly, Richard comes running into the room.

Before anyone can say anything, Gray jumps at him with a knife I hadn't seen before. He stabs him in the back and I hear Richard scream.

"Grayson! Stop! If you kill him I'll never get out of this cell! I'll die in here." The words somehow reach through his rage and he pulls away from him, looking at me. Richard is kneeling on the ground, a few feet from my glass cell. He is looking at me with a smug smirk still on his face, even through the pain.

"What do we have here?" he says the words through gritted teeth. He slowly stands back up and turns around to look at Gray. "Come to save the day, did we?" He laughs and I look at his shoulder blade where there is a knife sticking out of his now bloody button down.

"I won't let you take her, Richard." Gray has his jaw locked tight with anger. Instead of replying, Richard just laughs maliciously. He reaches into the back of his pants and pulls a gun out, pointing it right at Gray's head and my heart stops. *Why does everyone have a freaking gun shoved down their pants?*

"You do realize your expendable, Grayson? You mean nothing to me. You have no one who would miss you if my gun accidentally went off. I made sure of that."

"What do you mean you made sure of it? And you're wrong. I have Charlie and Ava and I'm going to save them both." Gray seems desperate as he talks.

"Richard." I try to get his attention but it doesn't work. He is staring at his nephew with his back to me. I think about shooting him myself, but I have a feeling this glass is bulletproof and I know my attempt would just make this worse. I already have a plan to save Gray and his sister.

"Richard! Look at me!" I am yelling again. Trying desperately to get his attention.

"You incessant little girl. What the fuck do you keep yelling my name for?" He finally turns his head to look at me. And when he sees the position I am in, his face falls.

I am standing behind the glass wall, staring out at both of them, with Gray's gun pointed directly at my own head. "I'll do it. I swear to you I will do it if you don't fucking listen to me." My threat seems to really get his attention now.

"Go ahead, Charlotte. Speak."

CHAPTER 25

Paxton

I walk into the big beach house I remember from my childhood. It's about 12 pm at this point, and the sun is shining bright through the windows. I told Gray to wait a few minutes, that I would leave the door open and he could sneak through once I had my dad distracted. I look back at him hiding behind a bush before I continue into the house. Hearing my dad's voice, I realize he is on the phone. I stop and listen for a second.

"What's your ETA, Mr. Santos?" He is quiet for a second. "That's great news! I respect a man who shows up early. She will be ready within the hour, out on the landing strip waiting for your arrival." He's silent again. "Yes, she is. I am sure you will enjoy her thoroughly. Now, if you will excuse me as I have other last minute arrangements to take care of with a buyer out in Spain." My fists are clenched so tight that I can feel my fingernails digging into my palms. How could he do this to innocent girls? Not just any girls, his own niece? The niece he raised as a daughter. I could kill him. But, that's not the plan. I need to calm down and distract him.

I put on my best drunk guy facade, and head into the big kitchen. My feet stumble against each other and I throw my arms up over my head. "Yoooo! Daddyo! What a small world!" I see the same two door fridge from years ago and walk over to it, grabbing a beer and popping it open.

My father jumps, looking over at me. "Paxton? What are you doing here? How did you know I was here, son?" His fake kindness makes me grit my teeth.

"I dunno. I wazz driving around and found myself here." I point down to the ground and then sway on my feet. "Shhhharlie won't talk to me. I's misssss hers sooo much and I needed to drink. Ssooo I brought a bottle of swhisky in the car and decided to drive to the beach. My memoriessss broughts me here and I saw your car outside." I hiccup and laugh hysterically.

"Oh Paxton, come sit down." He points to the couch and I stumble my way to him. The couch is facing the opposite direction of the basement door, so it's the perfect spot for me to keep my dad from looking that way. I fall down on the couch and then grab my dad's hand and pull him down with me.

"I love her." I know I'm acting, but the words feel so true when they come out. I do love Charlie. Even if I can't have her to myself, I love her so much.

"You deserve better than that girl Paxton. She comes from the wrong side of town. You'll find someone else who is worth your time. Someone who won't tarnish our name." I hate the words he speaks. He's such a pompous ass. How did I not see it all before? How was I so blind to this piece of shit? He puts his arm around my shoulder and I am torn between feeling comforted by the man I call my father, and being disgusted by the monster I know he is.

"She is amazingggg dad. Amazing." I see him start to fidget, clearly getting anxious. His knee is bouncing and he keeps darting his eyes around the room.

"You'll feel better once you're not drunk. Why don't you sleep this off and then we can go out to dinner later tonight? We can even spend the rest of the night here, together." He smiles a fake smile at me. He wants me out of the way so he can continue with his plans. He grabs my arm and helps me up. I purposely let him carry my weight, trying to slow him down. I know Gray is already in the basement, I saw him move out of the corner of my eye, but I want to give him time to get her. I let my dad bring me to the spare room that is on this level. He walks me over to the bed and I'm about to make a big scene, flailing around and saying I am going to throw up, when I hear something.

"Richard!" It's Charlie's voice screaming my dad's name. What the fuck? I stiffen at the sound and look at my father. His face is pale and angry.

"Sorry son." Before I can comprehend what is happening, he stabs a needle into my neck and everything goes blurry around me. Darkness takes over and the last thing I remember is hearing Charlie girl's voice yelling my father's name.

CHAPTER 26

Gray

"**G**o ahead Charlotte. Speak."

I watch as Richard stares at my girl. I watch the blood drip from his shoulder from where I stabbed him, the knife still sticking out. I wish I hit him right in the heart. I want to watch the life fade from his eyes. I want to feel his pulse stop beating under my fingers. I want him dead. But, Charlie is right. If he dies before I get her out of the cage, I may never be able to get her out of there. I have no idea how to open it. I wonder where Paxton is right now. He had to have heard Charlie scream. Please let him be okay.

I turn my attention to Charlie. She has a gun pointed at her temple. Her hands don't even shake as she holds the weapon to her own head. She looks confident and calm which scares me more than anything else. I feel the fear grip me like a vice as I pray to anything and everything that Charlie doesn't pull the trigger.

"Here's how this is going to go." Charlie's steady voice booms throughout the room. "You are going to let Gray go. You aren't going to kill him. And you aren't going to touch Ava. You aren't going to lay a finger on her. I will do whatever you want. I will figure out a way to get you even more money from this creep. I'll become a part of your business. You want a one-time money deal from this guy? How about a constant money flow? How about a deal where he shares me with his rich friends and colleagues. The American girl who doesn't have anything to live for anymore so she is willing to do anything. I'll convince him to give you 50% of the profits. Imagine that kind of money coming in every week."

My stomach rolls at the words coming out of her mouth. How can she say that about herself? How can she give herself up and succumb to such a horrible existence? The answer slaps me across my face. Because she loves me and wants me to be safe. She thinks if she gives herself up, Ava and I will be free. She thinks that will make me happy. But, I'd rather be dead and know she is safe than ever live a life without her. Especially knowing the pain she would go through every day.

"Charlotte, no." I make my words loud and final.

"Let the girl finish," Richard yells my way as he continues to point the gun at me. "Your offer is tempting darling. But, what if I say no?" He looks back at her and smiles.

"If you say no, I blow my brains out right here, right now. You disappoint a very powerful client, who will drag your name through the mud. It's your choice really. Hurt your name and lose money, or become more powerful by simply letting Gray live. I will walk out of this room with you, no questions asked. I won't put up a fight. I will get on that plane and you can get a deal set up with Antonio after I convince him of our little business idea. Trust me, I can be persuasive." She is suggestive with her words as she bats her eyes at the devil and I stare at the woman in front of me. This isn't Charlie. She is pretending to be someone she's not. I see the dead look in her eyes. She has given up on herself completely. She doesn't care what happens to her anymore.

"Oh, darling, I'm sure you can be real persuasive." Richard's voice changes and I can hear the arousal in his words. It makes me want to rip his throat out. "I like the way you think. I have a feeling we can make a deal. But, what if I want a little piece of the action before I send you away with him?" I watch the fear flash through Charlie's eyes at Richard's insinuation. It's there and gone within a second and then Charlie puts a fake smile on her face that wavers, ever so slightly.

"Whatever it takes to let Gray walk out of here. I want Ava and him safe, or no deal." She looks at me for a split second and the emptiness in her gaze steals the breath out of my lungs.

Gone is the girl I fell in love with, and in her place is just emptiness. Nothing.

"Charlie, don't do this. Stop, please. Please, baby, come back to me." I start to walk towards the glass wall and Richard gets close to me and stabs the gun into my back, hard. Charlie gasps quietly and it tells me that there is still a small piece of her in there. Somewhere deep down, my Charlie is hiding away.

"Do we have a deal?" Charlie's voice is loud and stern.

"Yes. We have a deal Charlotte." I let the sobs escape as I look into the eyes of the girl I love. I feel sorrow before I feel the anger consume me and then in a flash I turn to attack him. Before I can get my fist in his face, he puts a needle into my arm and laughs at me as I fall to the ground. I see everything happen in front of me. I can't move. I can't speak. But, I can see. Richard walks over to the opening where Charlie grabbed my gun and instructs her to hand it to him. She hesitates at first, staring over at me as I blink back at her, and then places her only defense into his hands. He places his palm on a certain spot on the glass and a scanner drifts down it before the glass wall opens up, freeing Charlie. I try to move, to help her, but I can't move a muscle. I feel the tears escaping from my eyes still. This has to be a nightmare. This can't be happening.

I watch as Richard grabs Charlie's arm and brings her over to where I am crumpled on the ground. He points the gun in his hand down at my head and then instructs Charlie to get down on her knees in front of him. No. No. Please, God, don't let this be happening.

"If you try any funny business, a bullet goes right between his eyes." He uses his other hand to unzip his dress pants and then pulls them down slightly. It's all happening right in front of me and I desperately try to move, to scream, to do something. But, nothing happens. I hear Charlie fall to the ground on her knees and it sounds painful. She looks down at me for a split second and the blank, hollow look in her eyes makes them appear almost black. She's gone. My sweetheart is gone.

She turns back to Richard and bends forward and I force myself to close my eyes. Refusing to watch this nightmare unfold before me. The tears are forming a pool of water around me as I hear Richard's deep groans and Charlie's quiet sobs echo through my head.

CHAPTER 27

Charlie

I'm standing on the private landing strip that overlooks the ocean. I can't stop staring out at the vast and calm sea. I imagine myself floating in it. Nothing surrounding me, consumed by the cold water and nothing else. It seems relaxing, until I realize that's exactly what I'm doing right now. I'm floating in an empty darkness inside my head. There is nothing else floating through my brain. No thoughts or fears. No memories of what just happened to me. What I just had to do to Richard. It's all blacked out, which I am so grateful for. But, this feeling isn't relaxing. It's suffocating. It's like my body wants to give up, but the blood circulating through it mocks me. The red liquid and pounding heart keeps my body moving, even though the rest of it is already dead and empty.

I look down at the outfit Richard made me change into. He watched me undress the entire time as I changed out of my dirty scrubs from the hospital and into the skin tight spaghetti strap mini dress. It was a dark crimson color, fitting really, and it barely covered my ass. The heels he put me in made it nearly impossible to stand up straight, let alone walk.

Richard is standing behind me as the plane comes into view in the air. He has a smile etched on his face and it's been there since we left the basement. I wait as a private jet lands on the landing strip and a bunch of men dressed in black button downs hop out of the plane as the stairs descend to the ground. I wait for my heart to start racing, but it doesn't; it stays at its slow, deafeningly loud pace. It almost feels disconnected from the rest of me. The men stand in two lines on either side of the stairs that now extend from the plane, three in each line, with their hands at their sides. I stand on the pavement, waiting for someone to say something, but they don't even make eye contact with me, let alone say anything. Suddenly, a man emerges from the plane and I focus my attention on him.

He's wearing what looks to be an extremely expensive black suit that stretches over his broad body. He can't be over thirty years old, with his dark black hair cut short, and smooth tan skin. His eyes are a dark brown color, almost black, and they get darker as he looks at me, if that were possible. He has a strong and sharp jaw line that clenches as he looks over me, eyes boring into my now soulless body. This is Antonio? He is not what I imagined.

"Mr. Santos, It's a pleasure to meet you." Richard speaks with confidence as he breaks the silence.

"Please, Mr. Santos is my father. Call me Mateo." His accent flows so smoothly through the air and I gulp. Mateo? This isn't Antonio?

"Well, is your father with you?" Richard questions him. This man hasn't stopped looking at me. He hasn't looked at Richard once, and I'm sure that pisses him off.

"He sent me to collect. I just wasn't aware *she* is what I was supposed to be collecting." He glares at me now and I feel my heart race for the first time since I watched Gray fall to the ground.

"Yes, your father is paying a great deal of money for this one. You were aware of what he has... business in, correct?" He is clearly annoyed that Antonio didn't come himself.

"Sim... Of course I am aware of my father's disgusting obsession." His accent comes out thicker as he looks me up and down, clearly angry. "He just didn't tell me I was going to be helping him pick up his little... prêmio. Otherwise I would have said no. What the fuck happened to her face?"

"She slipped. Are we going to have a problem?" Richard's voice is hard and clipped.

I watch as Mateo clenches his fists tightly at his sides. He appears furious and I think he might attack Richard, or send his guards after him. For what? I'm not so sure. Maybe because it appeared that Richard had tainted what belonged to his father.

"Nunca. My father will transfer the money. Let's go passarinho." He looks at me as he says it and I'm assuming whatever Portuguese word that was is in reference to me. I don't fight. I said I wouldn't. I walk forward, leaving this disgusting man behind me along with my Gray and Uncle Brian. I know I'll never see either of them again. But, as long as they are safe, I'm okay with leaving.

***

The jet is spacious and I find myself sitting in a comfortable chair across from Mateo. The inside is just as white as the outside. We have been on the plane for almost three hours now and neither one of us has said a word to each other. He keeps staring at me with his dark piercing eyes, as he drinks from his crystal glass. It has an amber liquid in it, and I wonder if it's the same Jack that my Uncle Brian gave us on my birthday. Doubtful. This stuff is probably ridiculously expensive.

There are eight other men on the plane besides Mateo. The six that came out, I'm assuming bodyguards, and then two pilots. There are also two women dressed in skimpy stewardess outfits who could very well be supermodels. They keep sauntering back and forth, swinging their hips as they watch to make sure Mateo's glass is always full.

"Passarinho, would you like a drink?" His voice startles me. I hadn't heard the deep voice and smooth accent in hours and it makes me jump.

"No." I am cold and distant. Refusing to look back at him as I stare out the window. "What does that word mean?" I don't know why I ask, but it keeps bugging me.

"What word? Passarinho?" I shake my head yes, stealing a quick glance at him. He has a devilish smirk on his face as he dissects me in my seat. I try to pull my short dress down, feeling his eyes on me. The movement only makes it ride up more and I see his eyes travel to where it slides up. I swear I hear a low, animalistic growl come from his throat, but I must have imagined it because he doesn't appear fazed or interested at all. He just flicks his eyes away, looking out the window, and taking a long swig of his drink. "It means little bird. It felt fitting."

"Why is that?" I try to sound strong, even though I am already completely broken.

"Because you're this fragile little thing, and you're flying away from home." His words swirl around in my mind. He is actually spot on, but I don't want him to think I'm weak.

"I'm not fragile. I just have nothing left to live for." The words leave my mouth before I can think twice about them.

"Hm. Sounds like you are about to break any minute now." His accent hits my ears.

"Well I'm not breaking." I'm broken, I think to myself. "I'm saving the people I love. I'm becoming your fathers little fucking pet so my boyfriend and uncle are safe. I have gone through more shit than you can imagine and I'm sure what's to come is going to be much worse."

Mateo stares me down. I can't decipher the look on his face. "Você é mais forte do que eu pensava." He takes another sip of his drink. "Boyfriend, huh?" The fact that he focuses on that makes me roll my eyes. I want to ask what he said in Portuguese, but it's not even worth it.

I don't bother answering him. I just look back out the window. I can feel his eyes on me and it scares me. At least, that's what I blame the shiver that runs through my body on. Fear. It has to be... right?

"Eu não vou deixar ele te machucar amor." His voice is slow and soft. I have no idea what he said but it sounds so beautiful that I try to memorize the way it sounded in my head. My eyes are back on his and he is looking at me with that strange look again. I should be asking him questions about what's to come. What his father is like. What my new life will be like. But no words escape my mouth. It's like my tongue is frozen in place. So, instead, I retreat back to the window and close my eyes, imagining Gray's blue eyes staring back at me. The scary part?

Every time I try to picture his eyes, I see dark brown piercing ones instead.

CHAPTER 28

Gray

I am still lying on the floor after what feels like hours. The room is dark and cold, and all I can hear are my own ragged breaths echoing through the damp air. I kept my eyes shut long after Charlie and Richard left the room. Long after he grunted loudly and Charlie whimpered for the last time. Long after I heard his pants zip back up and I felt another piece of Charlie's innocence fade into oblivion. He took this from her. She was supposed to do that when she was ready. When she was with someone who loved her completely. With someone she could trust.

Someone like me. She threw her entire life away for me. But I wasn't going down without a fight.

No. Fuck that.

My fingers and toes were finally starting to twitch when I pushed all of my might into the movement. After a little longer, I was able to turn my head slightly, squeeze my hand shut, and eventually, slowly sit myself up. My eyes were blurry from the tears that wouldn't stop. My hair was damp from their salty puddles where I lay. When I felt strong enough, I got to my feet and slowly made my way to the exit of this room that will forever be in my nightmares. I have no idea where Richard is, but I haven't heard anything since the loud engines of the plane. The plane Charlie is on. With that sick mother fucker.

"Paxton?" I manage to get up the stairs, but I have to crawl most of the way. "Paxton? Are you here?" A part of me is scared he is dead. I make my way around the house slowly, searching every room for him. But, he's not here. Did he fucking run? Did he just leave us high and dry after everything went down? There's no way. He wouldn't do that to Charlie... would he? I find his car outside in the driveway, but Richards is gone. Richard must have taken him. Why would he leave me here? He knew I would be able to move eventually. I don't dwell on the thought as I jump into Paxton's car. I put it in reverse and zoom down the long driveway. I'm on the road, maybe half a mile away when I hear a loud explosion. The vibrations that shake the car make me slam on the brakes. I look around to see where it came from, and find the source coming from where I had just left.

There is a huge, black mushroom cloud floating in the air exactly where the beach house resides. Well, where it resided. Richard blew up his house, and if I was paralyzed for another five minutes... I'd be dead.

CHAPTER 29

Charlie

"A mor, wake up." I hear a soft European accent through the black sleep that consumes me. "Estamos aqui." The words are deep and melodic. I feel a soft, warm hand rub my cheek, brush my hair back, and even touch my lips and I swear I swoon in my sleep. Why am I dreaming about a foreign man touching me? I reach out in my dream and find the strongest arm I've ever touched, pulling it towards me to cuddle up close. "Mmmm, Gray."

I feel the arm stiffen under me and then the voice talks again. "As much as I love listening to you moan, now is not the time, little bird. We are here. Time to wake up." Those words bounce around in my sleep ridden brain. It feels like a tennis match, going back and forth from one empty cavern of my brain to the other, until finally, it clicks into place. I'm on a plane to Portugal. This isn't Gray. This is a stranger. A handsome, older, scary stranger that is bringing me to his sick sex slave obsessed father. I gasp as I push away from Mateo and cower in the corner of the chair, as far from him as I can get. The gasp makes my ribs sear but I conceal the pain. He just chuckles softly at me as he shakes his head.

"Relax, amor. We are in Lisbon. It's time to see your new home." He reaches out for my hand, but I refuse to take it. I stand on my own, reaching down so I can put the small excuse of a dress I'm wearing back into place. My ass was definitely on display when I was sleeping, but that's the least of my worries. We are here. That means, I get to meet the man who owns me.

I walk behind Mateo, until we reach the exit of the jet. The moon is bright, but I can't see any stars in the dark blue sky. We are on a small landing strip and a cool breeze hits my barely covered skin, causing goosebumps to engulf my body. The breeze smells of fresh cut grass and it makes me forget for just a second why I'm here. It almost feels like a vacation, until I see an older man walking up to us. I avoid eye contact by looking at my surroundings some more. The landing pad is part of a huge estate. And, when I say huge, I mean huge. There is a mansion to the left of the landing pad, looking over the water. The house is lit up with a million twinkling lights, and I can just barely make out that it is white with an orange clay tile roof. There are huge arches and it has to be at least three floors high. Attached to the main house, if you can call it that, is a brightly colored building, just as twinkly and lit up. The building has similar arches but it is definitely a different color. Maybe blue or green? I can't tell. The landscaping is intricate, with lots of stone steps covering the rolling hills and what appears to be a huge perfectly manicured hedge maze. Not to my surprise, the maze is also lit up by beautiful twinkling lights. I have never been anywhere so magical in my life, and it makes me want to cry that I was dragged here to become some scary old man's toy. Life just isn't fair.

"Mateo, tenho estado à espera da sua chegada!" The older man's accent is thicker than Mateo's and his voice is gravely. "Esta é ela, não?" I can't understand a word he says, but I decide it's time to take a look at the man who bought me.

He is shorter than I expected, considering Mateo has to be at least six feet tall. His once dark hair is now salt and peppered with grays. He has thick eyebrows that need to be trimmed, and a small gut. Besides that, he appears to be strong for his older age. He has to be in his late 60's, maybe 70. The thought makes bile rise in my throat. There's no way I can do anything with this man. None. Not a chance. Nunca. I almost laugh at my use of the language, but then I remember the situation I am in.

"Yes. You forgot to mention I would be picking up one of your little play things, papai." Mateo speaks English and I can't help but wonder if it's for my benefit. Either way, I'm thankful.

"Sim sim. eu pensei ter contado-"

"English, papai. Speak fucking English." Mateo grates out. Antonio rolls his eyes and then looks at me with a revolting wink.

"I think I tell you that you pick up my American beauty. This is her, Mateo. The one from years ago. Charlotte." His English is subpar but I understand what he is saying. He glances at me again and his eyes take me in, before he smiles at me. My fear of this man makes me take a step back as I try to cover myself up, but I fail epically since I have a half inch of fabric covering my entire body.

"Ela é ainda mais bonita do que eu pensava," I have no idea what he said but the way he is staring at me is making my skin crawl. Mateo nods at his father but doesn't offer anything else. The look on his face has changed since his father said my name. He hasn't stopped staring at me with wide eyes.

"I'm going to take her to her room. She is injured, Papai. Ela está ferida. We need to let her sleep." Mateo's accent is so smooth compared to his father's rough tone.

"Ehh, okay. Take her to her room. I will see you both tomorrow." He is walking away but I can hear him speaking in Portuguese still. I can't make out what he says but one word stands out. Virgin. I feel my tongue get heavy in my mouth as saliva pools into it. I swallow it down, refusing to throw up.

"Let's go, amor. I'll show you to your room." He puts his hand on the small of my back and I don't push him off. Mostly because

I am too scared right now and he is the only person here who has shown me any type of kindness. But also because I can feel the warmth of his hand through my thin dress and it almost comforts me. We walk across the perfectly landscaped property. My heels are impossible to walk in so I am walking slowly and wobbly, even with Mateo's encouraging touch on my back. At one point, my ankle twists in my heel and I start to fall. Strong hands grab onto me, but those hands are holding tightly onto my broken ribs and the pain meds have completely worn off so I cry out in pain. Mateo puts me down on the ground quickly, letting go of my waist as he drops down to his knees.

"Little bird, what happened? Você está bem? Did you hurt your ankle?" He is frantically looking over my body. I just stare at him as I breathe through the pain in quick shallow breaths.

Who is this guy? Why does he seem to care about what happens to me? I belong to his father. He knew about his father's obsession with women, as he said before. I'm pretty sure he called me disgusting if I remember correctly. So, why is he showing me mercy?

"No. It's not my ankle. I'm fine." I try to push him away but he is stronger than me.

"What is hurting amor?" His voice is stern and it makes his accent come out even thicker.

"My ribs. I hurt my ribs back in America. I'm fine. I just overreacted. Let's keep going, I would like to go to bed." I pretend to be strong, but the real reason I want to keep going is because I just want to let the tears escape in private. I know I won't be sleeping. Mateo glares down at me and it makes the already present goosebumps on my body stick out even more. I hear a low growl before he grabs onto me and hoists me up. I expect his hold to be hard and painful, but his hands hold onto me with a gentle caress. He has me in a cradled position, with my bad rib away from his body. I avoid eye contact as we move, embarrassed that this stranger is carrying me like a baby, but I can't find my voice to tell him to put me down.

We move faster with me in his arms, making our way to the brightly colored building. Up close I realize the building is in fact a brilliantly bright baby blue color. I have never seen a house painted this beautiful hue before, and I can't help but let a small smile take over my lips. Mateo continues walking until we enter through huge glass double doors. All of the lights are on in the house and I let my eyes dance across all of the beauty in front of me.

We are standing in a great room with plush white couches filling the middle of it along with a large crystal coffee table. The floors are hardwood and there are cathedral ceilings detailed with intricate shapes and details that remind me of the maze outside. The walls are the most amazing part of the room. They are covered in art. A rich deep blue paint portrays a story across the walls with trees, old architecture, statues, and just random beautiful designs. I could stare at the walls for days and never get tired of it.

Mateo continues to walk as we go under an archway that is at least fifteen feet tall and enter into a hallway filled with the same royal blue pictures. He catches me staring, my eyes I'm sure are bugging out, and a smirk takes over his face. I feel my cheeks heat up and try to hide my now red face. We walk up to the first large arched white door to the left and Mateo opens it up. The walls in this room are gray with white tree branches arching every which way. There are small leaves adorning every inch of the branches and it's a breathtaking sight. There is a large four post king size bed in the center of the room with a plain white comforter that reminds me of a cloud. The room is huge, with two arches that lead into other rooms. One is to the right of the bed and one is to the left. The ceiling is just as high as the one out in the great room, with the same detailed design, but there's something different about this one. Right above the bed, at the highest point on the ceiling, there is a huge circular mirror that is at least ten feet in diameter.

What on earth is the point of having a mirror all the way up there?

Mateo chuckles deeply and it steals my attention off the mirror. "You seem quite interested in my ceiling, amor." I probably looked like a crazy person.

"I'm sorry. I just don't get the point of having a mirror on the ceiling." I don't know why I let the admission slip out. It sounds childish now that I said it out loud.

"Perhaps one day you will be able to see the point of such a mirror, Charlotte." His tone is lower than before and it makes me shiver. He feels it run through my body since I am still in his arms and I watch as something flashes across his dark brown eyes. His grip on my waist tightens just slightly, and I can't hold back the gasp that escapes my lips. He must think he hurt me again, because concern takes over his features as he carries me to the bed and deposits me on top.

Before I can move, or breathe, or talk, or think, Mateo grips the top of my red dress with both hands, right above my injured ribs, and rips the fabric apart as if it were simply paper. My dress is now lying completely open leaving me in the red lace strapless bra and matching thong that Richard made me put on. My scars are exposed and I feel like I could scream, but no noise comes out of my mouth. I know what comes next. Mateo is going to force himself on me. He is going to take advantage of me, just like his father will, and I can't do anything about it. Because I asked for this. I told Richard I wouldn't fight, as long as Gray and Ava were safe. So, instead, I close my eyes tightly.

To my surprise, I don't feel his hands groping me or hear him undressing. He doesn't rip off my underwear or pull down my bra. I peek open my eyes and find him standing there, looking down at me. He isn't staring at my bra or thong or legs, he is staring at my ribs. He is staring at the bruised and crimson letters that are etched into my skin. Anger and concern swirl around his dark irises.

"Eu vou matar quem fez isso com você." His words are filled with rage and protectiveness and I wonder what he said. I'm too shocked to ask though. He rushes off into the room to the left of the bed, that I realize now is a bathroom, with no door I might add. He is back by my side within seconds and holds a bottle of antiseptic and some cotton balls in his hand.

"May I, amor?" He tries to make his voice calmer. I just look at him in confusion and slowly nod my head yes. He tips the antiseptic bottle over onto the cotton to soak it before slowly bringing it to my skin. His eyes are on mine the entire time and I can't tell what burns more. The antiseptic searing into my open wounds, or his stare. There's something in his eyes that keeps holding me captive. I can't figure out what it is, but I have never been so transfixed by someone, or something, before in my entire life.

The burning in my side slowly fades away as he finishes wiping the vile word with the cotton ball. After he's done, he opens a small pill bottle and takes out two white oblong pills. "This is simply for the pain, amor. If you do not trust me, I will not force you to take them. But, they will help you sleep more comfortably." Something about his voice, and the way he speaks to me makes everything inside of me scream to trust him. I can't figure out why, but I find myself leaning up towards him and opening my mouth. He looks down at me and licks his bottom lip, letting his eyes fall on my half open mouth. His hand reaches forward and he drops the pills in, fingers grazing against my lips. The feeling is so intense that it hurts and I jump back from the sensation, as if it shocked me. I reach for the small cup of water he brought and swallow the pills down.

"Thank you," I say as I pull my gaze away from his and reach for a pillow to cover myself up a bit.

"De nada. I will grab one of my shirts for you to wear." Before I can protest. He walks over to the door to the right of the bed and comes back out holding a dark gray t-shirt and a pair of black boxers. "This should be more comfortable for you to sleep in. I will make sure you have more clothes for tomorrow as well."

I reach for the clothes and then stop halfway to them. "Is... Is this your room?"

"Sim, amor, it is." He doesn't hesitate with his answer.

"Why? Wh- Why am I in here? I thought I belonged to your father. That's what Richard told me at least. He told me I would have to do whatever Antonio wanted, whenever he wanted and I wouldn't have any say in the matter because he owns me completely. I figured I'd be thrown in a dungeon, forced to sleep with him right when I showed up, rub his feet, never be able to wear clothes again... have his babies... "The last one makes me cringe. "Shit like that. Isn't that what sex trafficking is? Why am I here with you? Unless you are trying to use me first before your father can get his hands on me. Which seems plausible, I guess. But if that's it, why haven't you just done it already? Why didn't you just fuck me right when you ripped my dress off? Why take care of my cuts and give me pain meds?" I'm spiraling down a hole and I can't seem to stop talking. The things coming out of my mouth would normally make me turn beet red in embarrassment but I can barely even tell what I'm saying as I go on and on. I'm about to continue, when Mateo comes over and puts his finger on my lips, telling me to stop talking. The contact shocks me again, but not as intense and I let him keep it there.

"Are you finished, little bird?" He tries to hide his smile, but I catch a glimpse of it. I simply nod my head yes. "First off, you will not be fucking my father. He wouldn't dare do that with you, and I would never let him touch you either way. He is a very gruff man, and I don't agree with his little hobby, but he is not interested in you in that way. Second, I want you to be comfortable and I know you will be in here. Those injuries are bad and I want you to heal. The other girls can be a bit... jealous, at times and I don't think throwing you to the wolves is the best idea." He lets his finger brush against my lip, dragging it down, bringing a shiver with it. "And third. I didn't just fuck you when I ripped off your dress because you're going to be begging me for it when I do the first time amor." His last statement is low and husky, and I gulp. What did he just say? I feel my whole body shaking from the nerves and maybe something else entirely. Keep it together, Charlie. This is a complete stranger and he could be lying to you. What interest could his father have in me if it wasn't for sex? None of this makes sense.

"Okay." Is all I give back. I stand up straight and try to appear as unaffected as possible. I realize after I said it that I pretty much just agreed to his last sentence and I back track. "I mean, um. Not okay like, you know. I'm not saying okay to me begging for you. I'm just... I said it cause. Okay." I give up and close my eyes tight, wishing I was less of a nervous wreck. I hear him laugh at me and it only makes me feel worse.

"You, meu amor, are adorable." I open my eyes to see him full on grinning at me. Like white teeth glistening in the light, lips curved up high, and dimples out for all to see grinning. It makes him appear younger and I can't help but smile back as I stare at him. "Eu poderia olhar para o seu sorriso para sempre." The sentence sounds so beautiful when he says it and I desperately wish I knew what he was saying.

"If I'm going to be staying here for, you know, the rest of eternity, I should probably learn the language right?" I don't mean for the question to sound like I'm asking him, but he takes it that way.

"Sim, little bird, I will teach you everything you need to know in time. But for now, you should get some sleep." He starts to walk towards the door and I find myself speaking up without meaning to. "Can you wait until I fall asleep?" I say the words quickly and it makes me sound like a child.

"Of course. Get in bed." He turns back around and walks toward the large bed. I pull the covers off and then get in and bring the plush blanket back on top of me. The bed forms to my body and I can't hold back the moan that escapes from how comfortable it is. The pain meds have definitely kicked in because I can't feel the pain in my side anymore. I hear Mateo's low chuckle at the other side of the bed and then realize he is sitting on top of the comforter. I try to hold back the smile that forms on my face.

"What did you say before, in Portuguese?" I close my eyes tight, wishing I didn't ask.

"I said, I could stare at your smile forever." His words make a spark engulf inside of me. I am still a shell of a person, but somehow Mateo is already bringing a glimpse of life back into me and I've only just met him hours ago.

I look down at the bracelet I am still wearing from Gray and feel tears cascade down my cheeks. I miss him so much, but a part of me is scared that the person I miss never even existed. I know he loved me, but I also had a feeling if it came down to choosing, I would never be his choice. I can't say I blame him. He doesn't have anyone left besides his little sister. But, I would have given up everything for him. In fact, I just did. I gave up everything for the man that tricked me into loving him. I gave up everything for the Uncle who brought me right to my captor. I still don't know if that part is true, but a part of me deep down knows it is. I have always been a nuisance to him, and I know his life will be better without me in it. I gave up my life to save the people I loved unconditionally, even if their love wasn't unconditional for me. But, none of that matters anymore. I will never see any of them again, and I'm sure they are relieved.

"Boa noite, amor." Mateo's voice breaks through my thoughts. I curl up around a pillow and take a deep breath. Mateo's cologne engulfs my nose and sandalwood and sea spray take over my senses. I feel myself getting heavier in the bed as a calmness blankets over me.

"Good night, Mateo."

CHAPTER 30

Uncle Brian

I don't know how to handle grief. I don't know what to do when something tragic happens. I don't know how to act, what to say, where to go. I simply panic and shut down. I have been crying in our dark shit hole of a house for what could be hours or days. Last I heard, Charlie was in the hospital and doing okay. That had been forever ago. At least it seems that way.

My chest squeezes at the familiar feeling I felt ten years ago. I can almost hear the officer's voice in my head. Telling me my sister and her husband were killed. Telling me Charlotte was gone. They couldn't find her. They searched for weeks, while I sat in my frat house and drank until I couldn't feel anymore. And even then, I felt too much. The day they found her I begged for custody. I begged to have the last piece of my only sister left. The last piece of my family. They, of course, didn't fight it since it was a better alternative to foster care.

I love that girl more than I have ever loved anything in my life. It broke me every day seeing the pain in her eyes. The grief and sorrow and death. She deserved the entire world, and all I could give her was a minimum wage lifestyle. She never asked for anything, but I always wanted to give her everything. Now she's hurting and I can't even get my sorry ass off the floor. I have a bottle of whiskey next to me. Well, it used to be a bottle of whiskey. Now it's just an empty glass bottle that oddly resembles exactly how I feel right now.

The sound of my front door opening should have startled me, but I'm so numb that I barely even notice it. That is, until someone is standing over me shaking my shoulders violently. "Fuck off." I have no idea who it is, but I'm in no mood.

"Brian, get up. Please." His voice sounds familiar. Why does it sound so familiar? I try to turn and look at him but my vision is blurry and the light makes me squint.

"You're fucking wasted? Are you kidding me? Brian, Charlie is gone. GONE!" he screams so loud that I jump. I actually feel something through the endless empty bliss my Jack has offered me. I start to sit up and the words this stranger said to me register. Charlie is gone. Yeah I know that. She's in the hospital. Because I couldn't protect her. Because those fuckers that hurt her the first time were never caught. Because the world isn't fair.

"I know she's gone dumbass. She's in the hospital with Gray. I failed her again. I always fail her. She deserves such a better life." Somehow the words almost sound coherent through my wasted sobs.

"Brian. Get your shit together!" The voice is still yelling at me. "I'm Gray. I'm right here. And Charlie isn't. She's gone. They took her again. They took her for good this time. She's not even in the country anymore." It takes me a good thirty seconds to comprehend the words that fly into my ear, but finally it clicks. She's gone? Like gone, gone? No. That's not possible.

I start to stand up. I stumble forward, catching my fall with my hands. I make another move to get up but a hand falls on my back, holding me in place. "I have to save her! I have to get Charlie back. I can't. I can't lose everyone. She's my everyone." My words barely make sense in my own head but I feel every syllable in my soul. As drunk as I am, I know I need to save her. I need her. She has saved me through all of these years.

"I know, but you aren't saving her in this condition Brian.

You need to drink some water, eat something. I'll make you some food and then we can talk. We are going to save her. I promise you that. We need to figure out how to get to Portugal. We need to save her from the hell she's in."

CHAPTER 31

Charlie

I dream of Gray all night. I feel his hands on me. His lips on my lips. His touch burning into my skin. His teeth grazing my earlobe. I expected nightmares once sleep blanketed over me, but this is a welcome distraction. I watch the movie play over the back of my eyelids. I watch as Gray looks down at me, his blue eyes sparkling with love and desire. I watch as he kisses me from my neck all the way down. I feel every brush of his fingers. Every swipe of his tongue. Everything. I watch as he lifts his head up and looks at me with his bright blue eyes. He smiles and says my name, but his voice sounds different. It sounds exotic and foreign. Suddenly, his blue eyes turn dark brown and the picture before me shifts. The man in front of me now has tan skin, and his black hair is styled perfectly. He smirks at me as he bends forward and places a kiss on my ribs. The contact makes my toes curl and I hear myself breathing heavily in my dream. I will myself to wake up as his name slips through dream Charlie's lips. He kisses down my ribs, slowly getting lower and lower until-.

I startle awake, breath labored and body tingling. I can still see images of my dream flashing through my empty mind. Shaking my head, I will the images away and look around. My eyes crawl across the beautifully decorated room until they land on a white chaise lounge in the corner. The chaise isn't what catches my eye, it's the second leading star of my dream that is sleeping on top of it that does. I start to stand up, noticing how wobbly my legs are. I quietly make my way closer to the chair, letting my curiosity of this man get the best of me. He is fast asleep, with one arm tucked behind his head and the other hanging off the side of the chaise. His mouth is hanging open, and his breathing is steady. I admire the way his normally perfect and intimidating face looks in this relaxed state; almost childlike.

Before he can wake up and catch me staring at him like a creep, I make my way over to the room I assume is the bathroom. I walk under the arch and am taken aback by the huge bathroom in front of me. The sprawling room is decorated with even more of the deep blue walls I have become accustomed to these past twelve hours. There is a deep white clawfoot tub that could easily fit three people next to the double sink, a large cubby-like room where a toilet resides, and the most intimidating shower I have ever seen. This thing is probably the size of my old room. It has a huge waterfall shower head along with four more adorning the two shower walls. Yes, I said two walls. Because besides those two cornering walls, the shower is completely open. There isn't a shower curtain or a glass shower door to provide any kind of privacy. Instead, there is a low ledge to sit on and the shower is facing the large bathroom mirror, making it impossible not to see yourself naked and showering. This guy clearly likes to look at himself.

I quickly use the bathroom before deciding whether a shower or a bath is a better idea.

The bath will take longer, but the shower scares me. Screw it, I might not have a lot of time before he wakes up and who knows when I'll have a chance to shower again. I find a towel in one of the cabinets, which is the softest and biggest towel I have ever felt, and quickly undress before hopping into the expansive shower. It takes me a few minutes to figure out how to work the damn thing, but finally, hot water cascades down from the ceiling and walls. I step under the steaming water and let it overtake all of my senses. My eyes close as the water drowns out everything around me. I bring my hands up to my hair and run my fingers through their wet strands. It feels so good, I almost forget where I am. That is, until I open my eyes and look straight into the mirror across from me. I see my tired eyes staring daggers into my own body. I see the painful bruises all over my ribs. The name that will forever be carved into my flesh.

The sight of who I have become is enough to make bile rise in my throat. I shut the water off and barely manage to grab the towel before running to the toilet and dry heaving into the bowl. I can feel the tears falling down my cheeks, but I make no attempt at brushing them away. Instead, I fall to the ground and lay in a heap next to the toilet, letting the cold tile floor numb the pain that comes with every breath. Letting the tears fall one by one, each drop a silent reminder of the life I have and the life a normal eighteen year old girl would be living. But I guess I've never been normal, have I?

"Charlotte? I'm coming in." I barely register his voice from the bathroom door. I don't move, don't speak, don't do anything but stare blankly at the ground as the tears just pour out. I feel his presence before I see him. I feel him behind me, his eyes taking in the pathetic scene before him. A crumpled excuse of a girl who has no family, no friends, no life to live, laying near a toilet, full of bile, barely covered up by a towel. The thought pulls a loud sob out of me and I hear Mateo say something in Portuguese behind me.

Warm hands touch my bare shoulders, but I barely feel them. Before I comprehend what's happening, I feel my body lifting off the ground and into the air. My body is again being cradled by the same strong arms. He carries me back to the bed and deposits my limp body onto the soft fabric.

"Amor, what happened in the bathroom?" His question is quiet and followed up by those same warm hands brushing through my wet hair. The feeling brings me back to reality enough for me to comprehend what he said.

"What happened? How can you even ask that?" The words are hushed but firm. "I wish I still had a family. I wish I had people who actually loved me. I wish I was back home, but I don't even know where home is. I wish... I wish I was dead." The last word hangs in the air between us. I feel him tense behind me.

"I thought you were strong, Charlotte. Remember when you told me that on the plane yesterday?" His accent is thick and his words are clipped. I sit up fast and glare at him after hearing what he said. Is he joking?

"Screw you. I gave myself up to save people who don't even love me. I willingly came here to be your father's property. You act like this sweet, caring hero when really? You are going to let him do whatever he wants with me. Just like you let him hurt all of the other girls you told me about last night. You're just as much of a monster as he is! You're worse!" I am screaming by the time I finish. I continue glaring at him as he stares back. His features change from concerned, to completely furious.

"I have been nothing but kind to you. You act so smart, passarhino, but you know nothing. You sit here and call us monsters because of lies that some dick in America told you? Not everything is as it seems Charlotte. Those girls I spoke of last night? They are here of their own free will. Yes, they may have showed up in an unsavory way, but my father has never forced himself on any of them or forced them to stay. He handles things wrong but he is not a monster. The monsters you speak of seem to be back where you came from if you ask me."

I'm speechless as I watch him move away from me and towards the door that exits the bedroom. I know I need to say something, but my mind is spinning in circles after what I just heard. "Mateo..." I get one word out and he turns around to look at me. "I... I..."

"I'm going to get you something to eat. And then I will bring you to my father." His words are cold and heartless. They make me shiver in fear at what's to come. He just told me his father has never forced himself on the other girls, and that if I wanted to leave I could. But why should I believe him? Yes, he has been nothing but nice to me. Yes, he seems trustworthy and kind hearted. But, I've been hurt so many times before that I can't trust anyone anymore. I can't even trust myself.

CHAPTER 32

Charlie

I try to keep track of where we are going as Mateo leads me from the blue house into the mansion. I watch as we pass through the huge double glass doors that lead into a large sitting room with twin circular stairs on either side. The walls are all white and there are mint green columns cascading from the twenty foot ceiling down to the floor. I barely have time to admire the room before Mateo leads me down hallway after hallway, turning left and right so quickly that I realize I couldn't escape this maze if I tried. We stop in front of a rectangular, dark wood door that contrasts against the white of the walls and soft arches of the other passageways. Mateo stops and turns around, acknowledging me for the first time since we left his room.

He looks me up and down slowly, taking in the dress he gave me when he brought me my breakfast. The cotton dress is powder white, hitting right above my knees. The sleeves reach my forearms and it has a cinched waist with buttons up the front leading to a delicate V-neck. It's much more modest than I expected. I figured I'd be put into something similar to the napkin I showed up here in. His eyes trailing my body sends shivers down my spine, all the way to my sandal clad toes. I was so grateful that I didn't have to put heels back on. I almost broke my ankle last time I had to put on those monstrosities.

"This is my father's office. Once you speak with him, I will take you upstairs to your room... and then to meet the other girls." His words make my heart race. I don't know what to expect and I am scared of every different outcome that my mind can think of.

"Can you..." I try to get the words out but my voice cracks with nerves. I look down at my sandals. "Can you come in with me?"

"Yes, Charlotte. I will come in with you. You may not be able to understand everything my father says so I will help translate when necessary." I don't miss the way he used my full name instead of any other nicknames he has called me.

Taking a deep breath, I nod my head for Mateo to open the door. He reaches for the handle and the door opens up. I dart my eyes around the room, taking in the dark brown walls, the many shelves filled with books, and the single mural of dark green plants taking up the wall behind a large desk. A large desk that is occupied by the man who owns me.

His eyes meet mine and what appears to be a genuine smile takes over his sharp features. He is less intimidating in the daylight. His eyes are the same color as Mateo's, maybe even darker. He motions for us to sit in the two chairs on the opposite side of his desk, the smile never wavering on his face.

"Meu Deus..." He takes a deep breath and I swear I see sadness flash across his face. "You look just like her." His words make me scrunch up my face in confusion.

"I look just like who?" I can't stop the words from leaving my mouth.

"Ah, you have no idea why you here, no?" He puts his elbows on his desk and clasps his hands in front of him.

"Richard told me... I mean, yes... yes, I do know. You bought me from Richard."

"Sim, I did buy you from that idiota. But, you know why?" I

feel both his and Mateo's eyes on me and my heart starts to race again. I don't answer, having no response to give.

Instead of talking, Antonio reaches for something on his desk. He grabs a picture frame that is facing him, and then passes it to me. The picture before me makes my breath catch in my throat. Tears form in my eyes and confusion consumes my brain.

I stare down at the woman in the picture frame. She looks just like my mother. Same wavy brown hair, same blue eyes, same sweet smile. The only thing different about this woman is the structure of her nose. Where my mom had a small button nose, similar to mine, this woman's nose was slightly broader and longer. She was breathtaking and the resemblance to my mother was uncanny. I barely notice the small boy holding her hand in the picture because I'm so transfixed by this woman, but when I look down at him I see Mateo's big brown eyes staring back at me. His boyish features remind me of him when he was asleep on the chaise in his room. He has a huge smile on his face, with his two front teeth missing. I can feel both of their happiness through the picture and it tugs at my heart.

"I... I don't understand. Who is this? She looks just like my mom." The tears start to fall down my cheeks.

"She looks like you too, Charlotte." Antonio's words have a hint of sorrow in them. "That is why you are here." His words make no sense in my mind. "Mateo, explain to her."

I look over at him and catch him staring at me. He's staring at my face with concern as he watches the tears drip down my cheeks. "This woman was my mother, little bird. My father met her in America when they were young and she moved to Portugal with him. They had me and were married for fifteen years before she passed away when I was twelve. Cancer took her from us." He swallows audibly and I catch the quick glare he gives his father before continuing. "My father has never been right since. He never moved on. He became obsessed with this idea that he could find someone to replace the love of his life. He came across the business of sex trafficking, paying for women, after years of simply searching the US for another American woman like her. He thought he could kill two birds with one stone. Find a woman who looked like her, and save as many women from living a life of hell." Mateo's voice lowers as he says, "I think it's fucked up. I don't agree with any of it but he thinks he's doing the right thing." I shake my head in understanding.

"He made it known the type of woman he was looking for: brown curly hair, blue eyes, light skin, and then people like Richard, started sending them his way. He offers a life for every single one of them. He offers money, a home, and if they want to leave, he helps them start a new life here. But so far, every woman has chosen to stay." He shakes his head, as if disgusted, before continuing. "None of the women resembled my mom more than your mother did. Richard sent a picture of you and your mother ten years ago and my father instantly saw the love of his life staring back at him. He asked Richard for your mom, but he told him what had happened... that your parents had been killed and you were the only one left. My father had no interest in children. He wanted to be with your mom, but seeing how much you resembled her made him obsess over what happened to you. He wanted to make a life for you, bring you here and raise you as his own... He told Richard that he wanted you, no matter what it took. When Richard said you had run away, my father worried for years about what had happened to you... until Richard called months ago and said that he had found you practically homeless with no one. He wanted to offer you a better life than what you had. So, that's why you are here." Mateo stops talking and the room grows silent. My laugh takes over the silence. I can't stop it from bouncing off the walls as the ridiculous story plays in my head.

"Passarinho? Are you okay?" The laughter finally subsides as Mateo and Antonio look at me like I have two heads.

"You expect me to believe that story? I loved my parents and they died because of people like you and Richard. I was living with my uncle and going to school before I was kidnapped, beat up, and almost raped so you could have me! Richard said you only wanted me if I was a virgin... explain that if you only wanted to 'help me'." I use air quotes for emphasis.

"Virgin? What does she mean by this, Mateo?" Antonio looks at him for answers. Mateo doesn't pay him any attention. He is staring at me. His eyes practically have visible flames dancing across them. His hands are white knuckling the chair and I swear if his jaw clenches any tighter his teeth will crack.

"Who is the one that beat you up and tried to-" He doesn't say the word. "Who did that Charlotte?"

"Don't act like you didn't know that already. You see my face, wrists, and ribs. Richard and his men kept saying they could do whatever they wanted to my body as long as they didn't take my virginity. They said that's all Antonio cared about. Well, good news! I'm still technically a virgin! Although I'm sure Richard would have gone farther than he did if it wouldn't have cost him millions." I'm blabbering again, unable to stop myself from talking. I hate how often I word vomit when I'm nervous.

"Se aquele filho da puta tocou em você." Mateo's words make the hair on the back of my neck stand up and I don't even know what he said.

"If who touched her, Mateo? Richard?" Antonio asks this in English, clueing me in on what Mateo said.

"Sim. Anyone who touched her is dead. Whoever Ronny is, Richard, anyone. I will kill them all." He sounds murderous and I have no doubt that he would do exactly what he said.

"Why do you even care? I don't understand what's going on here." I feel like I'm going to cry again from pure confusion. My head hurts from all of the different things swimming through it.

"Little bird, we are not the enemy. My father is not the best man in the world, but he had all of the right intentions with you. He wanted to save you. Richard is the sick bastard who couldn't understand my father's accent. He was trying to tell Richard that you look like my mom. That he wanted to save you. But Richard only heard what he wanted to hear. That's why he told you that you had to be a virgin. My mother's name was Virginia." He still looks enraged but as he says the name I see pain take over every feature in his face.

I'm speechless at this point. Could they be telling the truth? Are they actually trying to save me from the monsters I left back home? From people like Richard who killed my whole family and shipped me away just for power? People like Gray who made me trust and fall in love with someone who probably never existed in the first place? None of it makes any sense and I feel like I'm going to throw up again.

"Charlotte, I promise you can trust us." Mateo puts his hand over mine and the warmth engulfs my skin like an actual flame.

"How can I trust you?" I look at both Mateo and Antonio for an answer. Mateo sighs heavily as he looks at his father and then back at me.

"You can leave whenever you want. If you want to live somewhere else in Portugal or get on a plane right now and go back to America, we will let you. We will pay for everything. We will supply you with enough money to live comfortably for the rest of your life. We will…" He pauses and his jaw clenches. "We will stay away from you forever if that's what you truly want."

I'm about to say yes. That's what I want. I want to be brought back to America, even if there is a small twinge in my chest at the thought. But, Mateo speaks again before I can say anything. "Just know that you were surrounded by monsters back where you came from. The people that hurt you are back there. You are safe here. You have everything you could ever want and need. A home, money, an education, people who will care for you… we have cared about you for the last ten years and we had never even met you. We wanted you safe before we even knew you. Can you say that about the people you left behind?"

His words eat away at my thoughts of returning home. But one word catches my attention above the others. "We?" The two letter word makes Mateo look away from me, even as I desperately attempt to catch his gaze.

"Yes, Charlotte. We." His gaze finally meets mine again and my breath hitches at the intensity in their depths. His dark eyes stare at me almost begging me to say I will stay. "Just give us a few days to prove it to you, little bird. Give *me* a few days." I stare at him as his words sink in. He's asking me to stay. To let him show me what my life could be like here. I can't think straight. A half hour ago I thought I was sold to an evil sex trafficker who would destroy me. Now I'm finding out these strangers have cared about me for the last ten years and wanted to save me and help me make a new life for myself? It sounds even more insane after I say it in my head.

"I... I... I need to think. I don't know what I want." Mateo slowly nods his head in understanding. "I'm sorry."

"Charlotte, do not be sorry. We want you safe. We want to give you a good life." Antonio answers this time and I turn back to him. He still creeps me out. I don't like the idea of him buying women to replace his wife, but if he is bettering the lives of these women, and not forcing them to do anything, how bad could he really be? I am going to keep my distance from him no matter how long I end up here. "Faça com que ela fique na casa de hóspedes. Não quero que ela se preocupe com os outros." He looks at Mateo when he speaks.

"Sim, boa ideia." I understand enough to know that Mateo replied saying yes, good idea.

With that, Mateo stands and I take that as my signal to leave as well. I thank Antonio and follow Mateo quickly, before Antonio can tell me this is all some sick joke and I'm to be his sex slave after all.

"What did your father say back there?" I follow quickly behind Mateo, my head still reeling from the information I just learned. Mateo slows his pace without warning and my front slams full force into his hard back. I stumble backward, until his strong hands grab onto my shoulders to steady me.

"You are the clumsiest little bird I have ever met." His smile is wide, showing off his blindingly white teeth again. "My father said you should stay in the guest house. He doesn't want you to be overwhelmed by the other women in the house. I agree with him. é uma ideia fantástica."

"The guest house?" The thought of being away from all of the other women that apparently kind of look like me, should provide me with some relief. But, instead, the fear of being completely alone out here consumes me. "Where is that? I don't need to go somewhere else. I can stay with the others. I would rather be with them than somewhere completely alone." I fumble on my words, realizing that Mateo is still holding onto my shoulders.

"Is my passarinho scared?" The mocking tone is accompanied by a single perfect eyebrow raising. He gently squeezes my shoulders before continuing. "The guest house is the blue house we were in last night. You will not be alone. You will be with me." His thumbs now rub up and down my arms and the feeling engulfs my blood into a hot blaze, bringing a blush to my cheeks.

"Oh. I'm staying with you?" I say the words out of surprise, but realize they almost sound disappointed. Mateo notices, and he visibly stands a bit taller as he removes his hands from my arms. They leave a cold chill in their place.

"If you are not comfortable I can move into the main house for the time being. There are more rooms in the house, so you will have your own privacy, but if my presence makes you uncomfortable I will-" I cut him off before he can continue.

"No. I would appreciate it if you stayed with me. I was just surprised you would be willing to. I know how you feel about all of this. About the women your father buys." I look down in embarrassment, like I had something to do with this shit. Like I had any say in my own purchase. I feel warm fingers touch my chin before it is lifted up until my eyes collide with his.

"You are not like those other women, Charlotte. Get that through your head, okay?" His words are soft and all I can manage is to nod my head slowly, his fingers still resting on my chin. "Good. Now, let's go get you situated in the blue house. You can pick out your room and I will get us something to eat for lunch, sim?" I smile at his words and nod my head again before we walk back through the maze of hallways.

CHAPTER 33

Charlie

I've been in Portugal for almost three weeks now. My days have consisted of catching up on sleep, reading, Portuguese lessons with Mateo, exploring the grounds, and lots of eating. I mean, LOTS of eating. From decadent soups to fresh fish to pastries. Mateo even got me to try octopus the other day. The dish was called polvo à la lagareiro, which sounded delicious until the dish was put in front of me and I saw the actual octopus tentacles. I nearly threw up on the spot and refused to eat it. It got to the point where Mateo actually chased me around the dining room table with a fork in his hand. No surprise he's a faster runner than I am and when he got to me he held me down and forced the damn thing into my mouth. I hate that I liked the way it tasted. And I hate that I liked the way it felt when he held me down.

I've come to think of Mateo as a friend these past few weeks. A friend that I could stare at for hours. A friend that shows up in my dreams almost every night. He has been with me every day. I haven't met any of the other women here. I have watched a few of them out the great room window as they leave the mansion. They are always in groups, wearing fancy clothes, laughing and smiling, getting into expensive cars. When they come back they usually have shopping bags and perfectly done hair and nails. No part of me wants to meet any of them. Not a single cell in my body has any interest in being their friend. I am happy in my little bubble of the blue house and Mateo.

This morning is not unlike any of the last. I wake up in my huge king size bed. My room is right across from Mateo's and just as extravagant. The walls are white with the same royal blue art from the hallways. Only this art is designed in a wave-like motion, reminding me of the ocean that is right outside. There is a window the size of the wall that overlooks the crystal water and I find myself staring at its vast beauty more than once a day. I haven't ventured down there yet, but I am thinking about asking Mateo to take me today.

I have forced myself not to think about Gray or my Uncle Brian. It's been three weeks since I arrived here. It's ridiculous that I expected them to save me, but some part deep down hoped they loved me enough to try. I know how insane that sounds. I gave Gray an out. I made sure Ava was safe and that's all he cared about. He may have thought he loved me, but I know now that he was just fooling us both. It was a job to begin with, and he may have had some fun with me, but that's all I will ever be. A way for him to save his sister. I'm not upset with him for it. I probably would have done the same thing if the tables were turned. Hell... I did. As for Uncle Brian, I think me being away will make his life better. He can finally start a family of his own without his depressing niece holding him back. If what Richard said is true, he wanted me gone.

I will love and miss him forever but in the end, this will help him.

I sit up in bed and look down at the bracelet I still haven't taken off. *It's time Charlie. Take it off. You know deep in your heart you aren't going back there and you will never see him again.* I hate that damn voice. I hate how right she always is. I slowly slide the bracelet off and place it under my pillow. I don't plan on going back there. I don't know if I can stay here with Mateo and Antonio forever, but I know either way I will not be returning to America. I can start a new life here where no one knows the old me. Move into a place on my own, find a job, become a different person and start building myself back up. The thought is enough to bring a smile to my face as I jump out of bed. I look at the night stand and find exactly what I expect sitting on top of it. A new book that wasn't there when I went to sleep. I look at the cover and find the name *Darcy Coates* sprawled across the top. Another horror story. Mateo has been bringing me a book every night while I sleep since I told him about my obsession with reading romance and horror stories. I have a total of eleven books now and I have loved every single one so far. I grab the book and put it on the small shelf in the corner with the others.

After I shower in my private bathroom, I shuffle through the clothes that Mateo magically left in my closet after I picked out my room. I reach for one of the simple cotton dresses and then stop before I touch it. My fingers move to the drawer to my right and I open it up revealing 6 different bathing suits. Five of them are one piece suits and there is one single bikini that I have no plan on wearing anytime soon. My cuts and bruises have heeled since that night, but the word on my skin still scars me. I reach for a white one piece that has ruffley thin straps and a low back and step into it. Once I have it on I look into the mirror and try not to critique everything about myself. I have definitely filled out since being here. Any weight I lost during those horrible few days has been gained back thanks to the delicious food that Mateo is basically shoving down my throat. The bags under my eyes have disappeared and my hair falls down my back in smooth waves instead of the usual frizzy mess. I look at the tan that the hot Portuguese sun has rewarded me with and admire the freckles that have been enhanced by its blaze. If I didn't know any better, I'd say the girl staring back at me was happy. But I know better. As much as these past few weeks have helped me heal, I'm still empty inside. Mateo has brought fragments of me back, but I don't think I will ever be whole again. Pretending is the best I can do right now.

I quickly throw on a black cover-up that reaches my knees and walk out of my bedroom. The familiar smell of fresh toasted bread hits my nostrils. I walk through the great room and into the chef's kitchen that intimidates me every time I enter it. Mateo is standing with his back to me, preparing breakfast. I asked him one day if he had a chef, I mean look at this place, and he told me they have many, but he prefers to cook when he can. I walk up to the huge island and plop myself down on a stool.

"Morning." My voice makes him whip his head around and I am greeted with the smile I have grown so used to. "Bom Dia. How did you sleep, little bird?" He turns back to his food prep and waits for my answer.

"Good. Thank you for the book. I'm excited to start reading this one." I genuinely am. I love this author. Her stories always scare me enough that I start to forget about my own nightmares. "You're welcome. Maybe you can read it out on the patio today. It's un dia lindo." I look out the window and see the sun shining brightly. It is a beautiful day, but I don't want to read today.

"Actually, I was wondering if you were free? I wanted to go down to the water." Mateo turns back toward me, with two plates in his hands. They both have a huge piece of toast on them with cheese and ham. A breakfast I now crave every morning. He puts a plate down in front of me and my stomach instantly starts to growl.

"I would love to. Let's go down there after breakfast, sim?" He walks over to where two coffee cups already sit, full of the creamy espresso and milk I am now addicted to, and then takes a seat next to me.

"Thank you," is all I say before I dig into my meal and finish it within minutes. I feel Mateo's eyes on me and my cheeks heat up. He probably thinks I am disgusting. He probably thinks I've gotten fat and is repulsed by how much I have been eating. I push my plate away from me and start to sink down into my chair. That's it. I am going to start a diet today. No more bread and pastries. It angers me that Mateo can eat everything I eat, and then some, and still look as amazing as he does. I should start working out too. I'll ask him what his workout-.

"You look absolutely beautiful today, passarinho." His compliment halts my thoughts and somehow every insecurity I just felt flies out the window like it was caught in a large gust of wind. My cheeks burn hotter, but instead of embarrassment it's from something else. Something I refuse to look further into.

"Obrigada." I say, proud of myself for using the Portuguese word for thank you. Mateo simply smiles at me and slowly shakes his head with a light chuckle.

"You'll be speaking fluent Portuguese in no time, I'm sure of it."

"Well, my teacher is a pain in the ass who makes me study for hours every day so it better be getting me somewhere." I smirk back at him and take a sip of my coffee as his light chuckle turns into a full out laugh. The sound is like music to my ears.

"Alright smartass. How about we head down to the ocean, sim?" He stands and brings everything over to the sink, depositing the dirty dishes gently. I know there are maids, since everything is always cleaned up when we come back inside, but I have never once seen any of them.

***

We slowly walk down to the water following a stone path that gradually descends the cliff behind the estate. The view takes my breath away every time I see it. The blue water extends farther than the eye can see. The white sand lay perfectly still, letting the soft waves wash up on it. My toes tingle with anticipation at the thought of burying them into the warm white powder. We don't speak as we walk, but then Mateo breaks the silence.

"Are you happy, Charlotte?" His question surprises me and I

look up at his face. He is staring out at the ocean, but his eyebrows are furrowed in thought.

"Am I happy?" I repeat the question, mostly to myself to give me time to think of my answer. "Um. I don't know what I am. I don't know if I will ever be truly happy again. Not since my parents died... But I am more relaxed than I have been in ten years. I feel safer than I have ever felt. I made up my mind this morning actually." With that sentence Mateo looks right at me, awaiting my answer. "I don't want to go back to America. I can't. I left everyone behind and I know now that that's exactly what everyone wanted. I want to start a new life here. Become a different person and figure out how to live again." I look down in embarrassment at how pathetic my words sound.

"Passherino. You are perfect the way you are. Why would you want to become a different person?" His words ring in my ears. *Perfect.* That is not a word that should ever be associated with my name.

"I have so many issues that I need to figure out. Issues in here." I point to my head. "That have been eating away at me for years." I realize he probably thinks I sound crazy, but I don't elaborate.

"I understand, and I will be here to help you figure out those issues. I promise you." I look out at the ocean, getting closer to it with every step. How can he promise me such a thing? Why does he want to help me? I was supposed to be here for his father, and yet I have spent almost every second with Mateo and only seen Antonio a handful of times.

"Why?" The word is so quiet I doubt he heard it over the waves.

I hear him sigh. "Ten years ago I was sixteen years old. I felt like I was all alone in this world, grieving the loss of my mother. My father had lost his mind. I truly worried he was insane. He was obsessed over my mother's loss. He brought woman after woman to the house and I couldn't understand why. All I knew is every time I saw one of them, it was almost like seeing a ghost of my mother. I stopped talking to people, started doing bad in school, isolated myself from everyone. I felt empty." The fact that he says empty almost makes me stop in my tracks. He knows. "Anyway, one day I was walking past my father's office when I heard him crying. My father never cried. I saw him cry in the hospital with my mother when she passed, but that's it. I peeked in and saw him staring at a piece of paper in his hands. My curiosity got the best of me and I waited for him to leave his office and snuck in to see what he was crying about. When I picked up the paper I realized it was a photo. It was you and your mom. I saw her first, looking into the eyes of what looked just like my mom. Seeing her curly hair, her blue eyes, her smile. It made me sob, as I truly thought it was her. But, after staring for a bit longer, I noticed the small differences. The nose. The light freckles. It wasn't my mom. That's when I looked at the person she was holding in the picture. You. This small, perfect girl that had the widest smile on her face. I had never seen anyone so happy in my life. Your big eyes bore right into me and I swear something mended in my heart at that moment. I had no idea who you were, but this overpowering instinct to protect you took over. I wanted to make sure you were safe and that your smile never faded." He stops talking and looks at me, noticing the single tear streaming down my cheek. I wipe it away quickly, waiting for him to continue.

"My father told me about your story when I asked him about the picture. He told me what happened to your parents, how he wanted to save you... he said they lost you. I worried for years. My dad was only told that your name was Charlotte. Richard refused to give him a last name. He had no way to search. But, he told Richard that if he ever found you and you needed help, that he would pay him anything it took. Richard took that as him wanting you for different reasons and the money made him greedy. My father would never have taken you if he knew you were happy and safe. He cared for you. We both did, even though we can't really explain why.

"I eventually forgot about the girl in the picture. I moved on with my life. Got my grades up, went to college, started working in my father's Political world. The day I came to you in that jet, I had no idea what I was picking up. My father had never involved me in that part of his life. I walked out of that jet and the instant I saw you, I felt something deep in my chest that I couldn't explain. I still had no idea who you were, I had long forgotten about the little girl in the picture all of these years later. But, something in me knew, and the minute my father said your name, I swore I would protect you from anything and anyone. I will try for the rest of my life. You saved me from my own demons, and I plan to save you from yours."

I am speechless. Physically unable to say a word. How can I respond to such a story? What could I even say back to something so raw and emotional? He is clearly putting everything out there and I can tell it makes him uncomfortable. How could this man, all the way across the world, say that I helped him with his demons? I have been a nuisance to everyone in my life and somehow I saved this man without even knowing it? I'm so overcome with emotions that I still can't speak. So instead of talking, I do the only thing I can think of. I grab Mateo's arm and force him to stop walking. We are right at the edge of the sand, overlooking the blue water. I swallow my nerves and reach up, pulling him into an embrace. He doesn't even hesitate for a second. His strong arms engulf me and I'm surrounded by his scent, his warmth, and the sound of the waves crashing near us. He lifts me off the ground and pulls me in closer. He is holding me so tight, like if he loosens his grip on me I will disappear into thin air. The hug could have lasted for two minutes or two hours, I have no idea how long. Eventually, he places me back on the ground and looks down at me.

"Passerhino, I have wanted to hold you like that since I found out who you were." He strokes my cheek, wiping away a stray tear I didn't know had fallen. "I am here for you no matter what you decide. The only thing I am certain of is that I will protect you from anything that could ever harm you."

I think about his words for a second. I worry about my feelings for this man. He may have been searching for me for years, but when he saw that picture of me he was sixteen and I was seven. He saw me in a protective older brother way. He keeps saying he will protect me... is that all he sees me as? Just a younger sister he can take care of?

I stare at him with a smile but my mind is screaming at me that I'm in trouble. I can't deny the fact that I'm attracted to Mateo much longer. I have pushed these feelings down for the last few weeks, but every day, the attraction only gets stronger. *Oh Charlie. You really are an idiot.*

CHAPTER 34

Charlie

I t takes me about a half hour to finally take off my cover-up. The blazing sun was too strong and I had to get past my insecurities if I didn't want to burst into flames from the sun's rays. Little did I know, I almost burst into flames the minute my cover up came off. I felt Mateo's eyes on me and even though I knew he was simply looking to make sure my injuries were healed, a part of me hoped he was looking at me for another reason.

I walk into the ocean without looking back at him. I'm barely clothed and he is still in a dress shirt and pants. I feel too exposed. Wading into the water until it hits my chest I let the warm salt water seep into my skin and dig my feet into the cool sand. Turning around, I spot Mateo walking toward me and I swear the world stops spinning. His broad tan chest practically glistens in the sun as he makes his way toward me. His abs are perfectly sculpted and their hard ridges flex with each step. I am so transfixed by this man's body that I don't even notice the lack of pants he has on. Black boxer briefs. That's it. Barely leaving anything to the imagination. His eyes stay on me the entire length of his trip to the water. His face is so serious it makes my stomach flip from nerves. *Nerves, Charlie? Really? That's what we are calling this feeling?* My stupid inner voice mocks me, bringing me out of my trance.

I look down at the water as he approaches me and I swear the temperature of the water rises twenty degrees with his presence. He stops barely a foot in front of me and just stands there. Daring me to look up at him. I take the bait and look up, regretting it instantly. The heat in his eyes can't be mistaken. He is staring at me like a lion looks at his prey, ready to devour it at any second, but enjoying the game of toying with it. Letting it wonder when his killer will pounce. Giving it the smallest hope that it could possibly escape, even though they both know who wins this game. The predator always wins.

"Do you know what else I have wanted to do since I first saw you?" His words are low and husky. The anticipation of what he is going to say makes my body hum, but the fear that I am reading everything wrong niggles at the back of my mind. I can't speak, since my tongue decided to swallow itself from the mere fear of this predator. I simply shake my head no, at least, I think I do.

"I have wanted to kiss that perfect little mouth of yours since I saw you on that landing pad. I had no idea who you were at the time, but this overwhelming feeling that I needed to grab you and mark you as mine felt almost primal." See? I knew he was a predator. I stare up at him, waiting for him to say or do something. "I grew up wanting to protect you Charlotte. I had this instinct that I needed to keep you safe. But now? All I want to do is devour you. Will you let me do that, little bird?"

Speechless. This man makes me speechless. We are mere inches apart. I can feel his breath hit my skin as his nose just barely touches mine. My eyes flutter closed, and the lion takes that second to pounce on his prey. His hot lips crash into mine and everything goes black.

The world we live in no longer exists. The only thing I know is me and Mateo. His full lips pressed against my own. The salty taste of ocean water taking over my mouth. His kiss is demanding, yet softer than anything I have ever experienced. It is a combination of fear and safety. It feels like something I refuse to say out loud. But the word doesn't stop from running through my head over and over again as he explores my mouth with his.

Home.

CHAPTER 35

Charlie

I feel like I'm on cloud nine. Everything seems brighter as we make our way back up the cliff to the house. I still feel the empty hole in my chest, but this warmth that only Mateo can give me just keeps spreading through me like a small flame growing with every gust of wind. He grabs my hand halfway up the hill and that flame burns brighter.

I can't keep the smile off my face as we reach the estate. I am about to tell Mateo that I've decided I want to stay here for a while when I hear commotion coming from outside the mansion. I hear people yelling in Portuguese. Mateo notices as well and we rush over to the cause. He tells me to stay behind as he runs ahead of me. I should listen, but something pulls me forward. Something pulls me toward the yelling. Toward the men in black button downs that I know are the guards. I walk slowly, hearing the shouts, not being able to understand a word they say. Is that someone speaking in English?

As I approach the scene I see that two guards are holding a man down to the ground. Whoever this man is, he must be strong if it takes two guards to keep him down. One of the guards punches the man in the face. I can see the blood splattering from the hit and it's enough to make my stomach lurch.

"Please...." I hear the man's pained voice and something about it makes the hair on the back of my neck stand up. I move faster, finally getting close enough that I can see everything clearly. The sight before me stops my heart.

There are two guards kneeling on a disheveled man covered in blood. His clothes are ripped and I can just make out the tattoos on his chest. *No. It can't be.*

I step into the clearing and see his face. Even with the swelling and blood taking over his features, I could never mistake his face. His dark messy hair. His blue eyes. He looks at me for a split second and I hear a barely audible whisper leave his lips before he passes out.

"Sweetheart."

The End

EPILOGUE

Paxton

3 Weeks ago…

My whole body feels heavy as I slowly open my eyes. My mouth feels fuzzy and dry and my arms and legs are asleep. I look around, trying to figure out where I am, but nothing looks familiar to me. I'm sitting in a huge room full of bunk beds, the bedding perfectly tucked in. There is no one in sight, so I try to stand up and find my legs shaky and weak. What happened to me?

I slowly walk over to the door at the end of the room and find a bathroom. Walking toward the sink, I stare into the mirror and my stomach sinks. My head is completely shaved. I am wearing a full camo Army uniform. What the fuck is happening? I walk back through the door and search for someone.

"Hello? Is anyone there?" I'm screaming at the top of my lungs. "Please, someone help me!"

I watch as a man, at least 6'5" and 300 pounds of pure muscle, struts toward me with a murderous look on his face. I start to back away, in fear that he is going to attack me. He gets so close to me that when he speaks his spit hits my face.

"Private if you don't shut that damn mouth I will shut it for you!" He is yelling at me so loud my ears ring.

"Where am I? What's going on here?" The fear is overwhelming.

"You, Mr. Whitlock, are at the Fort Sill, Oklahoma Army Basic Combat Training Base. Now get your shit together!" He is still screaming at me. Before I can answer, he walks away from me and I hear his low, evil chuckle echo through the room.

How did I end up in the Army? The last thing I remember is going to save Charlie and then...

Fuck.

I'm going to kill my dad.

DON'T MISS OUT!

Book 2 of the Briar Series coming soon!

Stay updated on my website:

glstrongbooks.com

ABOUT THE AUTHOR

Gillian Strong

Gillian Strong is the author of When a Rose Falls, the first book of the Briar Series. She is a part time author, part time Real Estate Agent, and full time mom of a beautiful two year old girl. Living in North Eastern Pennsylvania with her husband and daughter, she spends late nights writing, taking advantage of the peace and quiet! in her free time, she loves to read romance and horror books, cook anything and everything, and spend quality time with her family.